My Beloved

War Torn Letters Series, Volume 3

Lexy Timms

Published by Dark Shadow Publishing, 2019.

This is a work of fiction. Similarities to real people, places, or events are entirely coincidental.

MY BELOVED

First edition. August 21, 2019.

Copyright © 2019 Lexy Timms.

Written by Lexy Timms.

Also by Lexy Timms

A Bad Boy Bullied Romance
I Hate You

A Burning Love Series
Spark of Passion
Flame of Desire
Blaze of Ecstasy

A Chance at Forever Series
Forever Perfect
Forever Desired
Forever Together

A "Kind of" Billionaire
Taking a Risk
Safety in Numbers
Pretend You're Mine

BBW Romance Series
Capturing Her Beauty
Pursuing Her Dreams
Tracing Her Curves

Beating the Biker Series
Making Her His
Making the Break
Making of Them

Billionaire Banker Series
Banking on Him
Price of Passion
Investing in Love
Knowing Your Worth
Treasured Forever
Banking on Christmas

Billionaire Holiday Romance Series
Driving Home for Christmas
The Valentine Getaway
Cruising Love

Billionaire in Disguise Series

Facade
Illusion
Charade

Billionaire Secrets Series
The Secret
Freedom
Courage
Trust
Impulse
Billionaire Secrets Box Set Books #1-3

Branded Series
Money or Nothing
What People Say
Give and Take

Building Billions
Building Billions - Part 1
Building Billions - Part 2
Building Billions - Part 3

Change of Heart Series
The Heart Needs
The Heart Wants
The Heart Knows

Conquering Warrior Series
Ruthless

Counting the Billions
Counting the Days
Counting On You
Counting the Kisses

Diamond in the Rough Anthology
Billionaire Rock
Billionaire Rock - part 2

Dominating PA Series
Her Personal Assistant - Part 1
Her Personal Assistant Box Set

Fake Billionaire Series
Faking It
Temporary CEO
Caught in the Act
Never Tell A Lie
Fake Christmas
Fake Billionaire Box Set #1-3

Firehouse Romance Series
Caught in Flames
Burning With Desire
Craving the Heat
Firehouse Romance Complete Collection

For His Pleasure
Elizabeth
Georgia
Madison

Fortune Riders MC Series
Billionaire Biker
Billionaire Ransom
Billionaire Misery

Fragile Series
Fragile Touch
Fragile Kiss
Fragile Love

Hades' Spawn Motorcycle Club
One You Can't Forget
One That Got Away

One That Came Back
One You Never Leave
One Christmas Night
Hades' Spawn MC Complete Series

Hard Rocked Series
Rhyme
Harmony
Lyrics

Heart of Stone Series
The Protector
The Guardian
The Warrior

Heart of the Battle Series
Celtic Viking
Celtic Rune
Celtic Mann
Heart of the Battle Series Box Set

Heistdom Series
Master Thief
Goldmine
Diamond Heist
Smile For Me

Highlander Wolf Series
Pack Run
Pack Land
Pack Rules

Just About Series
About Love
About Truth
About Forever

Justice Series
Seeking Justice
Finding Justice
Chasing Justice
Pursuing Justice
Justice - Complete Series

Kissed by Billions
Kissed by Passion
Kissed by Desire
Kissed by Love

Love You Series
Love Life

Need Love
My Love

Managing the Billionaire
Never Enough
Worth the Cost
Secret Admirers
Chasing Affection
Pressing Romance
Timeless Memories

Managing the Bosses Series
The Boss
The Boss Too
Who's the Boss Now
Love the Boss
I Do the Boss
Wife to the Boss
Employed by the Boss
Brother to the Boss
Senior Advisor to the Boss
Forever the Boss
Christmas With the Boss
Billionaire in Control
Billionaire Makes Millions
Billionaire at Work
Precious Little Thing
Priceless Love
Gift for the Boss - Novella 3.5
Managing the Bosses Box Set #1-3

Model Mayhem Series
Shameless
Modesty
Imperfection

Moment in Time
Highlander's Bride
Victorian Bride
Modern Day Bride
A Royal Bride
Forever the Bride

My Best Friend's Sister
Hometown Calling
A Perfect Moment
Thrown in Together

Neverending Dream Series
Neverending Dream - Part 1
Neverending Dream - Part 2
Neverending Dream - Part 3
Neverending Dream - Part 4
Neverending Dream - Part 5

Outside the Octagon
Submit
Fight
Knockout

Protecting Diana Series
Her Bodyguard
Her Defender
Her Champion
Her Protector
Her Forever

Protecting Layla Series
His Mission
His Objective
His Devotion

Racing Hearts Series
Rush
Pace
Fast

Reverse Harem Series
Primals

Archaic
Unitary

RIP Series
Track the Ripper
Hunt the Ripper
Pursue the Ripper

R&S Rich and Single Series
Alex Reid
Parker

Saving Forever
Saving Forever - Part 1
Saving Forever - Part 2
Saving Forever - Part 3
Saving Forever - Part 4
Saving Forever - Part 5
Saving Forever - Part 6
Saving Forever Part 7
Saving Forever - Part 8
Saving Forever Boxset Books #1-3

Shifting Desires Series
Jungle Heat
Jungle Fever

Jungle Blaze

Southern Romance Series
Little Love Affair
Siege of the Heart
Freedom Forever
Soldier's Fortune

Spanked Series
Passion
Playmate
Pleasure

Spelling Love Series
The Author
The Book Boyfriend
The Words of Love

Taboo Wedding Series
He Loves Me Not
With This Ring
Happily Ever After

Tattooist Series

Confession of a Tattooist
Surrender of a Tattooist
Heart of a Tattooist
Hopes & Dreams of a Tattooist

Tennessee Romance
Whisky Lullaby
Whisky Melody
Whisky Harmony

The Bad Boy Alpha Club
Battle Lines - Part 1
Battle Lines

The Brush Of Love Series
Every Night
Every Day
Every Time
Every Way
Every Touch

The Debt
The Debt: Part 1 - Damn Horse
The Debt: Complete Collection

The Fire Inside Series
Dare Me
Defy Me
Burn Me

The Golden Mail
Hot Off the Press
Extra! Extra!
Read All About It
Stop the Press
Breaking News
This Just In

The Lucky Billionaire Series
Lucky Break
Streak of Luck
Lucky in Love

The Sound of Breaking Hearts Series
Disruption
Destroy
Devoted

The University of Gatica Series

The Recruiting Trip
Faster
Higher
Stronger
Dominate
No Rush
University of Gatica - The Complete Series

T.N.T. Series
Troubled Nate Thomas - Part 1
Troubled Nate Thomas - Part 2
Troubled Nate Thomas - Part 3

Undercover Series
Perfect For Me
Perfect For You
Perfect For Us

Unknown Identity Series
Unknown
Unpublished
Unexposed
Unsure
Unwritten
Unknown Identity Box Set: Books #1-3

Unlucky Series
Unlucky in Love
UnWanted
UnLoved Forever

War Torn Letters Series
My Sweetheart
My Darling
My Beloved

Wet & Wild Series
Stormy Love
Savage Love
Secure Love

Worth It Series
Worth Billions
Worth Every Cent
Worth More Than Money

You & Me - A Bad Boy Romance
Just Me
Touch Me
Kiss Me

Standalone
Wash
Loving Charity
Summer Lovin'
Love & College
Billionaire Heart
First Love
Frisky and Fun Romance Box Collection
Beating Hades' Bikers

Watch for more at www.lexytimms.com.

My Beloved

USA TODAY BESTSELLING AUTHOR
LEXY TIMMS

Copyright 2019

ALL RIGHTS RESERVED. No part of this publication may be reproduced, stored in or introduced into a retrieval system, or transmitted, in any form, or by any means (electronic, mechanical, photocopying, recording, or otherwise) without the prior written permission of both the copyright owner and the above publisher of this book.

This is a work of fiction. Names, characters, places, brands, media, and incidents are either the product of the author's imagination or are used fictitiously. Any resemblance to an actual person, living or dead, events, or locales is entirely coincidental. The author acknowledges the trademarked status and trademark owners of various products referenced in this work of fiction, which have been used without permission. The publication/use of these trademarks is not authorized, associated with, or sponsored by the trademark owners.

All rights reserved.
My Beloved – Book 3
War Torn Letters Series
Copyright 2019 by Lexy Timms
Cover by: Book Cover by Design[1]

---

1. http://bookcoverbydesign.co.uk/

War Torn Letter Series

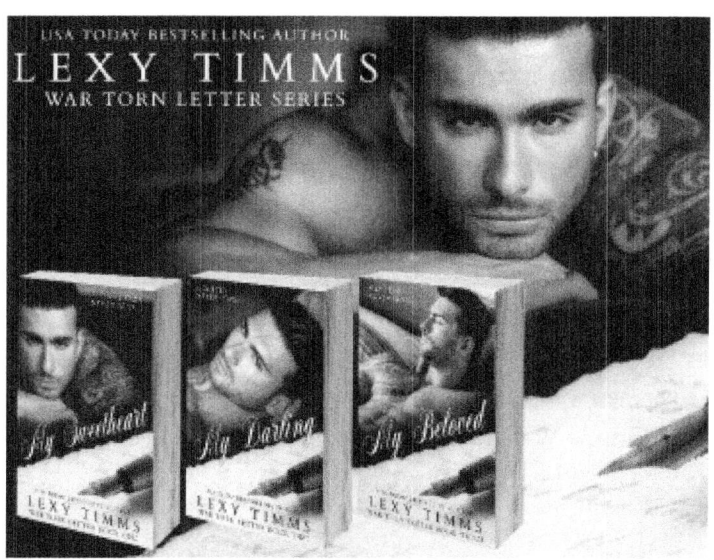

My Sweetheart - Book 1
My Darling - Book 2
My Beloved – Book 3

Find Lexy Timms:

LEXY TIMMS NEWSLETTER:
http://eepurl.com/9i0vD
Lexy Timms Facebook Page:
https://www.facebook.com/SavingForever
Lexy Timms Website:
http://www.lexytimms.com

Want to read more...
For **FREE**?
Sign up for Lexy Timms' newsletter
And she'll send you updates on new releases, ARC copies of books and a whole lotta fun!
Sign up for news and updates!
http://eepurl.com/9i0vD

My Beloved Blurb

You have to know the past to understand the present.
MONTANA. THIS IS WHERE the love story ends. This is where they found answers to the letters.

Except Amelia and Dane don't know if this is Claire's Thomas—or if he will want to go back to Pinewood to meet Claire.

Claire has no idea what Amelia and Dane are doing either. This could all blow up in their faces.

While they chase this fairytale, they're creating their own love story, and no matter what happens, they'll have their own happy ending.

But Claire has secrets she's been hiding for a long time, and Thomas harbors anger and bitterness.

Only time will tell which way things go. Will love find a way? Or is it possible for true love to die, after all?

Chapter 1

Thomas
Present Day

THE INCESSANT SQUEALING of the alarm clock on my nightstand pulled me out of a deep sleep and I reached across, slapping at it a few times until I found the snooze button. Or the cancel button. Or whichever I managed to get. It was silent again and that was what I was after.

I took a deep breath and let it out slowly. My breathing felt heavy, like there was fluid in my lungs, these days. The doctors had told me it was nothing to worry about. But wait until they felt like they were drowning, then we could talk again.

What bothered me more than the idea of getting old—the watery feeling in my lungs, the ache in my joints, the old man I didn't recognize that stared back at me from the mirror—was the hollow feeling in my chest. But that didn't come with old age.

I had felt this emptiness inside me since the end of the war.

Pushing myself up in bed, I could hear my bones click and creak as I moved. I swung my legs down to the floor and walked to the window, drawing back the curtains. It was still early, and I always woke up at the crack of dawn. The sun was not yet above the horizon, but the promise of a new day hung in the air, with purples and pinks coloring the inky night sky.

After relieving myself in the bathroom, I climbed into the shower, holding onto the railing that my nephew had installed for me. It made me feel like an old man to need that kind of thing, but the truth was that my body wasn't what it used to be. Damn, it hadn't been what it used to be since after the war.

So many times, my sister had told me that I should just consider myself lucky to be alive, even if I was a little broken and battered for it.

But had I ever really been alive? Was this living?

I shook my head, ridding myself of the thoughts before I thought about the answer, because I knew that every time I asked myself the question, the answer was no.

My life was empty, incomplete. I wasn't living. I was surviving. Not dying. That's not the same as living.

If I had to think about the reasons why, I was just going to make myself more depressed and I couldn't afford to fall into a slump. Not now that I was completely alone. There was no one here that would pull me back up, no one that would help me get through it. If I didn't get myself through this darkness, I wasn't going to make it.

Wasn't that the damn story of my life?

No, I couldn't afford to be so negative.

I climbed out of the shower, dried myself off and walked naked to the closet to find clothes to wear for the day. I looked at my body in the mirror. I was wrinkled, old. There were only traces of the strong and fit soldier I had once been. But my body was riddled with scars. Scars from the war where shrapnel had entered my skin, where knives had sliced at me, where bullets had ripped me apart.

Slowly, I ran my fingers over my scars, feeling the thick ridges of scar tissue, looking at the canvas of the man I had become.

I turned to the closet and dressed in faded jeans and a thick flannel shirt. I pulled on heavy boots and put a hat on my head.

Walking through the ranch house, I saw the photos of my sister and brother and their children adorning the walls.

There were no photos of me as I had grown older. No photos of anyone else, or of a family of my own.

In the kitchen, I fixed myself eggs and bacon the way I did every morning, making strong black coffee. I sat down at the massive wooden table in the middle of the kitchen when my breakfast was ready.

This kitchen was almost the largest room in the house. This table was the biggest I had ever seen. It had been bought like this, decorated like this, generations ago and it had been to host massive family meals. This ranch house had never been intended to be so quiet, and visited only by the ghosts of the past.

How long had it been since I had hosted a family dinner of my own? I tried to calculate. It must have been years ago, before my nieces had moved to the big city with their new husbands and their new lives.

Of course, I still saw everyone around Christmas. My sister came to visit, my nieces and nephews filled this house with laughter and joy for a short while. But I never had the energy to put up a tree if it was only going to be for a few hours, and no one cooked in the kitchen any more, my nieces always brought dishes along with them.

I barely saw my family anymore, really. I loved my nieces more than anything, and loved how my nephews had grown up to be strong men. But these days I only saw them when they had time to squeeze in a visit.

Of course, it made sense that they had busy lives, and things they had to take care of. Everyone moved forward.

Everyone but me.

After breakfast, I walked into the living room and sat down in front of the television. I should have headed out already to take care of the ranch, but I felt heavy today. Heavier than usual. And I didn't want to watch the sunrise on the porch. Once upon a time, it had been something I loved. But now, the sunrise and its beautiful colors only brought me pain.

As soon as I flicked on the television, the movie preview started. I was riveted to the screen, to the way that they told the story these days.

The action was so fast paced, the effect so extremely believable. It was nothing like back in the day, when television had only just been invented and the black and white images had had no sound to accompany them.

Oh, how times have changed.

As I watched the preview, my heart rate picked up. This was a war movie. My palms started to sweat and my throat went dry. I swallowed again and again.

Immediately, I was bombarded with flashbacks of the war. The sound of thunder in the air, created by bullets rather than the weather. The whistle of bombs falling all around us. The taste of mud and blood between my teeth.

I could feel the pain in every scar on my body as if the wounds had all been ripped open again. I could feel the trickle of blood on my skin, the warmth seeping into my clothes. I remembered the freezing nights when my teeth had chattered so hard I could barely hear myself think, when I had been frozen to the bone and thought I would freeze to death.

I saw Harry's face, so bloodied and mangled that I couldn't see his blank eyes staring up at me.

And the faces of so many other friends and fellow soldiers. There had been so much blood spilled on those battlefields, so many lives lost. And for what? There had been peace for a long time, now. There hadn't been another war of that magnitude. Sure, the world was still fighting, but nothing as serious as it had been back in the day.

What had it all been for? I knew that peace had finally been found, Hitler had been stopped and those who survived had been freed. But it felt like the price we had paid was too great.

Trying to shake off the thoughts and memories, I knew I couldn't afford to go back there, to be sucked into the nightmare of the past. If I didn't pull myself out, call myself back onto my feet, I was going to spiral down into a pit of madness.

Because that was what the war had done to us. I had heard of men who just hadn't been able to recover. They hadn't been able to bring themselves back. They had lost their minds, the very people they once were had been stolen from them. I was one of the lucky ones that had survived. Yes, I wasn't the man I had once been, but I was a hell of a lot closer than some other people I had heard of.

No, my life was empty and broken in other ways.

Switching off the television, I stood up. I had to get out there and manage the ranch. There was so much to do, especially now that I was the only one to run it. Sure, I had ranch hands to help me, but there was so much that still needed to be done.

And getting into the work would distract me from the memories, the flashbacks.

The house was eerily quiet, and it was during times like these that I wished I had people around me again. I yearned for laughter between these walls, and the happiness that had once lived here. It had been so long since I had been alone.

A knock on the door ripped me from my thoughts and I frowned.

Who the hell would visit me at this time of day? It was barely eight o'clock in the morning, if I was correct. Or maybe earlier, I wasn't sure. It was so easy to lose track of time these days.

It was probably a neighbor, come to remind me I had fences to fix. The dam cows ripped up my fences almost every day. Seems like we ought to be able to make a better fence.

I ignored the knock. The neighbors could come back later. I was going to head out to inspect the perimeters in about an hour, anyway. I would get around to it.

Again, a knock sounded and I groaned. Was an old man ever going to be left in peace?

But how could I complain? Hadn't I had just said that I didn't want everything to be so damn quiet? And now someone was here to interrupt the silence for me. But I knew it wasn't going to be someone who would light up the dark corners of this house. It was only in my dreams that things like that happened.

"Coming," I called in a gruff voice. I turned around and walked toward the door. It took me longer than it used to, just getting there. My legs felt stiff, my knees rickety. My steps seemed to be getting shorter every day.

How long was I going to be able to carry on doing this? How long would I be able to carry this load alone?

But I knew it wasn't because I was old and needed help that I felt like giving up. It was because of the heavy feeling in my gut that would never go away. It was because I was so aware of the loneliness, the emptiness around me, and I wondered how long I would last.

Finally, I reached the door. Sliding back the locks that I secured at night, I was already rehearsing in my mind what I would say to apologize to the neighbors for whatever had gone wrong. After all, I was just an old man. These things happened. I would do my best, I always did what I could.

Slowly, I swung open the door.

Chapter 2

Dane

THE PLACE WAS BEAUTIFUL. From the moment we had arrived in Stevensville, everything around us had been breathtaking. But this old ranch was on a whole new level. I could see why newspaper articles had been written about it. This was the type of place you would be proud to pass down through the generations.

Amelia and I had gotten up for breakfast and tried to spend as much time dawdling as we could before coming out here. But we had just been too excited, and Amelia had reasoned that if they were running the ranch, they would be up early anyway, so we wouldn't be imposing.

I had agreed because I hadn't been able to hold out any longer, either.

The ranch was only a short drive from the bed and breakfast where we stayed, and as we traveled, I had again been in awe of how the sun colored the fields around us, breathing life into the scenery that had become inky and silvered during the night.

Now, standing on the porch, with silvered wood beneath my feet, I knew why Thomas would have fought so hard to get back here.

The ranch house itself was spectacular, a double story house with windows that all seemed to be turned toward the rising sun, as if the house itself was basking in the glory of the nature around it. It hadn't been painted. Instead, the wood was only treated so that it looked as raw and natural as it had ever been.

The fields surrounding the house were lush and thick with green grass despite the changing of the season. In the distance the horizon was dotted with cows or horses. I couldn't quite tell from so far away.

When the breeze picked up it smelled like fall, but even more than that. Fall, wheat and happiness. This was the type of place you dreamed of. It was the place my grandmother had dreamed of for years and years.

I could see why. Thomas must have told her all about how it was to be here, how beautiful it was, and how it completed you. And it was this promise of happiness that she had held onto for so long, then mourned the loss of for the rest of her life.

"This place is huge," Amelia whispered, as if someone could hear us and it would be rude, but there was no one around, not for miles. I wondered how many people lived here, or if it was just Thomas himself. If it was, it would be doubly tragic. That he had come home to live out his life all alone.

"I can't believe how big it is," I answered. "Look, over there, do you see that?" I pointed and Amelia looked in the direction. The next ranch was almost three miles away, the house so small it looked like a toy house on the horizon.

"Yeah?" Amelia asked.

"That's the closest neighbor."

She turned and looked around again, shaking her head slowly.

"After growing up in the city, and then being in a place as small as Pinewood, this is just blowing my mind."

I smiled at her. I loved how she was in awe of everything she saw.

Amelia turned to me. Her face was suddenly tense, her brows knitting together, her lips pursed.

"What is it?" I asked.

"I'm so nervous," she whispered again. "What if he's not here? What if this isn't the right ranch? What if he's dead?"

I shook my head. "I know, I know. I feel it too. But we can't think like that." I pulled her against me. "We came all this way to find answers, and the only way to find them is to keep going. We'll know as soon as we're on the other side of that door."

Amelia nodded and wrapped her arms around me for a moment. I could feel her breathe in with a shudder and slowly let it out again.

I didn't show it, but I was nervous, too. I was scared that this would be the end of the line. That we had found Thomas Brown's ranch only to learn that he had died. But just as I had told Amelia, we were almost there. Soon, we would know if this was the end of the road or not.

Lifting my hand, I knocked on the heavy door.

We waited for a moment. There was no sound. Birds cawed in the distance and I heard the bleating of a cow, but other than that, there was no sign of life.

"Maybe try it again?" Amelia asked. "He's old, it might just take him some time to come to the door."

I nodded and knocked again. We waited again, and I was almost ready to give up when a raspy voice called from inside, letting us know he was coming.

"Oh, my goodness," Amelia said, looking at me with bright green eyes, biting down on her lip. My heart beat in my throat. This was it, I thought. This was the moment of truth. The bolts on the door slid back slowly, and then the door swung open.

An elderly man stood in front of us. He was a little hunched over but it wasn't hard to see that he was a tall man, with a square frame. He had thick gray hair and a beard covered half his face. Despite his age, he looked well-put together. His hair was combed neatly to the side, his beard was trimmed and his flannel shirt was tucked into his jeans. He had glasses perched on his nose and he looked like he could be anyone's loving grandfather, not a soldier who had been ripped up during the war.

"What are you kids doing here?" he asked. He was a little salty, but it was early on a Sunday morning. He didn't look like he'd just climbed out of bed, but it was still supposed to be a day of rest. As much as a ranger could rest.

Amelia glanced at me.

"Are you Thomas Brown?" she asked.

The man nodded when he looked at her and I swear he softened when she offered him the widest grin even I had ever seen.

"Why do you want to know?" he asked, his voice still a little gruff. But no one could be angry with Amelia.

"We've been looking for you," she said. "You have no idea for how long."

Thomas frowned. "What for?"

"Well," Amelia said, and she wrung her hands. Her nervousness was back and she glanced at me as if for support. And I would give it to her. I took over.

"Sir, I am Dane Peters," I said.

"Is that supposed to mean something to me?" Thomas asked.

Amelia put her hand on my arm. "Sir, Dane is Claire Whiteside's grandson."

We watched his face. He stared at us for the longest time, his face expressionless, his dark eyes moving between me and Amelia. We didn't say anything and just waited for him to respond.

What if he didn't know who she was? What if he'd forgotten? Or what if he wasn't even the right Thomas Brown? So much could go wrong and he stood there staring at us as if we had grown extra heads.

"Mr. Brown?" Amelia asked carefully.

"Claire Whiteside?" Thomas asked.

We both nodded.

And then his face crumpled a little. "Oh my... I hadn't thought I would ever hear that name again."

He scrubbed his face with one hand. I wasn't sure if the reaction was positive or negative. He could still chase us off his property.

"Claire," he said, as if more to himself than to us. He looked past us, his eyes glazed over and I knew he wasn't here. He was somewhere else. Somewhere far away, across the ocean.

"It's taken us so long to find you," Amelia said again, and her voice was gentle. Maybe she understood what was going on in his mind and heart. I had never experienced love the way Thomas and my grandmother had, or the way Amelia believed in. I felt out of my depth reaching out to Thomas when he looked like he had been transported away from us to a different time.

Reaching out, Amelia reached out and touched Thomas on the hand. His eyes slowly drifted back to her. He was still as put together as ever, but something about him had turned hazy. He was emotional.

"Can we come in?" Amelia asked. "We have so much we want to talk to you about."

Thomas stared at her for a moment longer, before he finally nodded and stepped aside. I noticed that his movements were slow, albeit precise. We walked into the house.

It was as spectacular on the inside as it was on the outside. The furniture was all old, probably the type of antiques Amelia would sell in her shop. And the house was large and decorated with fine taste.

"Please, sit down," Thomas said, leading us to a large living room with couches huddled around a giant fireplace. "I'll put on some coffee. It's been the longest time since I've had any company, let me tell you. Please, forgive the state of the place."

The house was nearly immaculate.

"I'll be right back," Thomas said, and shuffled out of the room.

When we were alone, Amelia turned to me, her eyes glittering with excitement.

"We found him, Dane!"

I nodded and kissed her. It was a quick kiss, just our lips pressed together. But passion flared up between us and when I pulled away, she looked at me with so much adoration I wanted to grab her and do it again.

"Can you believe we came this far?" I asked, instead.

"I really thought it might just be another dead end," Amelia said.

We were talking quietly so that Thomas wouldn't overhear us.

"He didn't look angry about Claire, the way she looked about him," Amelia added. "I think this is a good thing. I have a good feeling."

I nodded. I felt the same.

"Can I offer you kids anything to eat?" Thomas asked, coming from the kitchen. "I don't have much by way of food for the moment, but I have biscuits. Homemade by my neighbor. My sister used to do it, but now that she moved away, Martha has filled the gap for me."

Amelia smiled. "Biscuits would be great," she said. "Thank you, Mr. Brown."

He waved his hand at her. "Please, child, call me Thomas."

She smiled at him. "Thomas," she said, and the name was beautiful rolling off her tongue. She had a way of making everyone feel so special around her. But in their own way, as if they each had a special place in her heart. And Thomas was a man we had dreamed of and spoken about for so long, we might have only barely met him now, but he had a special place in our hearts, as well.

"I'll bring it," Thomas said. "Please, make yourselves at home."

He disappeared again and Amelia and I sat down on one of the couches. We looked around at the photos on the walls. Photos of women and children, and more photos of them grown up, older. I wondered if any of those were his children, if he had moved on with his life the way Claire had tried to.

Eventually, Thomas came back with a tray loaded with cups and bowls.

"Let me," I said, jumping up and taking it from the old man. I set it on the coffee table, still allowing him to offer sugar, milk and biscuits.

It felt so right to be here. So homey. Not only because we were here with the very Thomas Brown we had searched for all this time, but because being here felt like it could be home.

I understood why my gran had liked him so much. Thomas had something very welcoming about him once he got past being gruff about strangers intruding on his grounds.

Amelia made small talk while he prepared our coffee cups and I listened to her chat away, sounding so comfortable.

She always made me feel like I'd just come home when I was with her. Like I was exactly where I was supposed to be. Just as my grandmother must have felt about Thomas. I wondered Amelia felt the same way about me.

When she glanced at me, she had a look on her face that suggested she felt something. Maybe not exactly the same thing, but something all our own.

Chapter 3

Amelia

THOMAS BROWN WAS A beautiful man. It was easy to see that he was a man of integrity, upright and proud, even though he was hunched over by old age, and dragged down by everything he had been through. His face was worn, and he moved somewhat stiffly, as if something always hurt. But there was something about him that was fascinating.

I tried not to stare.

Part of me still couldn't believe that we had done this, that we had found him. I had been terrified that this would be a dead end.

But, apparently, miracles did happen. Ever since I had found that letter, it seemed like miracles had happened one after another. I had met Dane and was really starting to fall for him. We had found Claire Whiteside, against all odds. And she had finally told Dane enough about her past that we had now found Thomas Brown.

It was impossible to think that we were sitting here, on the ranch in Stevensville, waiting for the old man to make us coffee.

Dane sat next to me and he seemed relaxed. I was still nervous that something could go wrong, but what could happen? We had found Thomas, and he hadn't shut us down when we had spoken about Claire. Instead, he had invited us in and we were going to talk to him about everything. In fact, he had seemed excited. Emotional.

When Thomas came back with the tray filled with coffee and biscuits, Dane jumped up and took it from him. I looked at Dane, so caring and respectful, and it only made me like him more. I had seen him in such a controlled environment and I still really knew so little about him, it was wonderful to be able to see a different side of him. Travelling together had really opened up my eyes to another side of Dame, a side that I was attracted to just as much as the person I had gotten to know in Pinewood.

"I have to say, you kids are the last people in the world I expected to come knocking this morning," Thomas said, sitting down in an armchair that looked like it was his usual spot. "I mean, obviously I didn't expect you, specifically. But this news—" He broke off, looking emotional again. I leaned over and squeezed his hand.

I couldn't imagine how much this was to deal with, to take in. They hadn't seen each other for more than fifty years.

"We are sorry for coming over unannounced," Dane said. "Perhaps we should have called."

Thomas shook his head. "No, I think this will do. So, tell me about her. How is she doing? Where has she been all this time?"

"In a town in Oklahoma named Pinewood," I said, answering Thomas's question. "It's a bit of a long story, actually. And an interesting one." I glanced at Dane who smiled at me. When I looked at Thomas, with his coffee cup in his wrinkled hands, his dark eyes fixated on my face, I knew that this was the kind of story he would love.

"I work in an antique store and we get boxes of old items from time to time, boxes that people drop off because they don't know what else to do with the stuff. In the bottom of one of the boxes, I found a letter. A letter written to you, by Claire, in nineteen forty-five."

Thomas frowned. "A letter I never received."

I nodded. "When I read it, the love in it was so passionate, so strong, I just had to find the writer. It was in my quest to track down Claire Whiteside that I met Dane, her grandson."

Dane reached over to me and squeezed my hand. Meeting him was one of the happiest moments the letter afforded.

"It took us quite a while to track you down, too. At first, I thought it would be impossible. But we couldn't give up. I just had to know how this story ended."

Thomas sighed. "It didn't end very happily, I'm afraid. I came back for her, after the war. But she wasn't there anymore. She was gone."

"And we know why," Dane said, taking over. "She was whisked away to Oklahoma where she married an American named Reggie Peters."

At that, Thomas frowned. "An American," he said, and there was bitterness in his voice.

"Her father pressured her to do it," I said. I didn't want Thomas to think that Claire had intentionally abandoned him. I could only imagine how much that news would hurt, and it wasn't true. "She didn't have a choice, he wanted her out of the country during the war."

Thomas nodded slowly and I wondered what he was thinking, what was going on in his head and heart.

"You should know, Thomas, that she never loved Reggie," Dane said.

I looked at Dane. This was the first I had heard of it. Dane had told me a couple of things that Claire had told him, but there were still pieces of the puzzle that were missing to me.

"She was brought to America by a man that would supposedly take care of her, and at least she was safe. But she never cared for Reggie, and he never cared for her. After leaving England, Claire was doomed to a loveless life, doing nothing other than surviving, taking care of the house and the family."

It sounded awful. My heart went out to Claire. I couldn't imagine what it had to be like to marry a man I didn't love, to spend a lifetime going through the motions because there was nothing else to do. I tried to imagine the emptiness in that.

Dane continued talking about his grandmother and I was riveted, just as Thomas was. Most of the things he told Thomas, I hadn't even heard.

As Dane talked, I watched Thomas as well. While Dane explained the life Claire had lived, I noticed that Thomas was becoming emotional. His eyes became watery and his face crumpled a little, his breathing trembling while Dane spoke. When Dane finally stopped, Thomas let out a shuddering breath.

"She was supposed to wait for me," he said. He looked over Dane's shoulder, as if he had been transported to another place and time. His eyes were a little glazed again as they had been when we had stood outside on the porch, mentioning Claire's name for the first time. "I went back for her, you know. I went back to find her, just as I had promised. She should have been waiting for me. She promised me she would. She should have been there."

My heart broke for the old man. Imagine going back to find the love of your life, to fulfill your part of a shared promise, only to find the promise had been broken and that the love of your life was gone. I tried to imagine what it would be like for me to go to find Dane after he had promised to be there for me, only to realize that he had left me behind.

The ache was unbearable and it wasn't even something I had experienced. How much worse was it for Thomas who had lived his life knowing that Claire had left without him?

"If it's not too personal," I said, and Thomas looked at me. "Did you ever marry or have children?"

Thomas shook his head. "I couldn't," he said and his voice cracked a little. "Claire was the only woman I had ever wanted, and she was gone. And after the war, I was a broken man. My body was riddled with shrapnel, my mind wasn't what it used to be, and nothing of the future I had planned was left. I tried to find her, but in a world so vast, it was impossible. Eventually, I gave up and came back home."

Thomas took another deep breath and I watched as he pulled himself together. How many times in his life had he had to do that?

"My brother fell ill shortly after the war. Cancer got him. So I had to do what needed to be done to keep the ranch from going under. There wasn't time to think about a lost English girl, or to nurse a broken heart."

This was all so awful. I hated stories that didn't have a happy ending. I was so upset that Claire and Thomas hadn't found each other, and that they had never gotten their happily ever after.

"I am so sorry this happened to you," I said to Thomas. I wish things had gone differently."

"Me too, child," Thomas said. "Me too."

"But they still can," I added. "It's not too late."

Thomas looked at me with a frown. Dane looked at me with an encouraging expression, his lips almost curling into a smile, his eyes bright with anticipation. This was what we had come all the way here for. This was how the story was supposed to end. It was tragic that Thomas and Claire hadn't found each other. Tragic that she had been ripped away from her happiness by a man she had never loved, and that Thomas had been left behind mourning the loss. But it wasn't supposed to end this way. The story wasn't finished yet—if it didn't end happily, it hadn't ended. I knew that it might be a lot to take in, and that the news would all be a bit of a shock to Thomas. But I didn't want to wait. And I knew that Dane didn't want to wait, either. We were too invested in this, too excited. And we were all too aware of how precious time was, and how quickly it was running out.

Thomas sat in his armchair, his coffee long forgotten and his face a mixture of emotion. I knew that it had to be a lot to deal with, especially since he hadn't expected any of this. Just like Claire, he had been blindsided. But love had caught both of them unaware the first time. Why couldn't it all happen again?

And this was right. Dane and I hadn't worked so hard and searched for so long just for it to be over. There was still one last leg left of this journey, one last chapter to the story. And the upside was that now, Thomas was in control. There were no questions anymore, no variables. And as soon as he understood that, I was sure that he would feel exactly the same way about it that Dane and I did.

Still, just before I broke the news to Thomas, I felt a little uncertain. It was such a big step to take, such a wild thing to do. And so much time had passed, these two people had become settled in their lives, even though it hadn't been together.

But sometimes, to find true happiness, we had to step out of our comfort zones. It was something I was learning with Dane, something I knew he was learning with me, too. And now, I wanted Claire and Thomas to have the same happiness I felt when I was with Dane.

I reached for Dane, taking his hand and interlinking our fingers. I took a deep breath and looked at the old man again.

"Thomas," I said, looking at the old man again. "Do you want to see Claire again?

Chapter 4

Claire
1955

IT WAS EASTER. SOMEHOW, the last four months had flown by extremely fast and I was in the kitchen, preparing Easter dinner as I did every year.

But for the first time in more than a decade, I wasn't miserable.

In fact, I was almost happy. Almost.

After Reggie had come home on New Year's Day, everything had changed. It hadn't gotten to the point where I was brimming with happiness, but Reggie was really making an effort to meet me halfway on most things, and I was doing the same for him. We owed it to each other to be kind, to be thoughtful, and to take each other into account, even if we didn't love each other. After all, we were married. We shared a house. We were building a life together, the future.

Even if it wasn't what I had wanted. This was who I was now, this was my reality. Embracing it was easier than fighting it every step of the way. It had taken me so long to realize this, but finally, I was in a better space.

The house smelled like the food I had been cooking and music played, music Reggie had chosen. It was jazz, music that I really didn't care for, but it gave the house a happy feeling and we all deserved that. It had been far too long since I had been happy at all.

I heard Junior laughing in the living room. He and Reggie were doing something together. I wasn't sure what, but I was relieved that they had some kind of relationship now, too. In Reggie's attempt to do more, he had gotten a little more involved with Junior. And it seemed to be good for both of them.

I didn't even think about the fact that Reggie wasn't Junior's biological father. At this point, it didn't matter anymore. After all, if Reggie did what a father should, and Junior could look up to him, that was all that mattered. I was the only one that would walk around with this dark secret forever. And for the sake of maintaining the peace and making sure my child was happy, I would gladly do it for the rest of my years.

Despite being happier these days, I was still a little resentful of the fact that I was expected to cook and clean and maintain the house like a domestic worker. I wasn't a fan of the American Dream that Reggie chased day in and day out. I didn't like having to be caught up with laundry and cleaning and cooking and fussing over everything. But since things were better than they had ever been between us, and Junior was happy, it was a small price to pay. Besides, what else was I going to do with my time? I could barely remember what hobbies I used to have, or the girl I had once been.

Shortly after, Reggie's parents arrived. Thank goodness his brother Larry and family were back in Texas. I didn't think I had what it took to entertain them again. I really struggled having to bite my tongue with Reggie's family. But I had learned how to tolerate his parents, and since we saw them very often, it was a good thing.

"Hello, darling," Reggie's mother said, coming toward me with arms outstretched. But she didn't really touch me, didn't hug me. Instead, she stood right in front of me and clasped her hands together.

"I'm glad to see that the house looks a little better than the last time I was here."

I clenched my jaw and forced a smile. "I am glad to see that you're well. How have you been?"

I had discovered it was helpful to get Reggie's mother talking about herself. Then I could relax instead of trying to measure my words. She went on and on about something she had bought a short while ago, something that I absolutely had to swing by to see.

Though I was barely listening, trying to contain my bitterness.

Not long after, we all sat down at the dinner table. I had laid out the food in the middle and we passed plates around, allowing everyone to dish up.

"How long did you cook the chicken, dear?" Reggie's mother asked me, after finally taking a bite.

"Is it a little dry?" I asked, trying to keep my smile in place.

"Oh, don't be too hard on yourself. Chicken can be very tricky to master."

That was it. I saw white. I was so angry, I could snap. Why was what I did never good enough for her? Why was it acceptable that she tore me apart like this, in my own home, time after time?

"Excuse me," I said politely and stood, walking to the kitchen. If I didn't remove myself from the company immediately, I was going to say something I would regret.

Clearly, I was never going to meet their expectations. I was never going to be the wife they wanted for Reggie. Though I had known it from the start, it wasn't any easier to swallow.

I braced my hands on the kitchen counter, hanging my head low, taking measured breaths. I had to get through this day, I just had to focus on smiling and being as controlled as I could until they left. It wouldn't take too long, would it? I had no idea how long they would stay. Sometimes, Reggie's parents could hang around for hours.

So I just had to keep breathing like this, and keep smiling. That was all.

It was the only thing I could do, anyway

I heard someone coming into the kitchen, and a moment later, Reggie stood behind me. I turned around and faced him.

"I don't know how much longer I can do this," I said honestly. "She's never going to stop tearing into me. I am never going to be good enough for her."

Reggie stood a little closer and put his hands on my shoulders. His touch was gentle. Lately, he had been touching me more, even though we hadn't exactly been affectionate. I liked that he reached out to me, though. It was better than nothing.

"Just let it roll off your back," he said.

That upset me just as much as what his mother had done.

"It's not that easy, Reggie. Sometimes, I can take it. Sometimes, I understand what she is going on about. But sometimes, it's just too much."

I took a deep breath and let it out with a shudder, trying to keep it together. I had a lump in my throat and I felt like I was going to fall apart if I didn't bite back my tears now.

"You're going to get through this," Reggie said.

You. Not we. It was never us in this together. It was always just me, the one that had to endure everything alone.

And I'd had enough.

"You know," I said, opening a can of worms that I knew was going to cause trouble. But I couldn't help myself. "Sometimes, it would be really great if you could stand up for me."

I watched Reggie shut down on me and he moved back a step, letting his hands fall off my shoulders.

"Don't act like I'm the villain in the story."

I shook my head. "I didn't say that. But we are husband and wife. You're supposed to stand up for me. You're supposed to help me when I am being attacked like that, help me put this bullshit to an end."

"Language," Reggie scolded me.

Of course, that was what he was going to focus on. Not the fact that I was asking him for help. Not the fact that I needed him to be by my side. Reggie was only ever worried about appearances and I had to be the perfect little wife, I had to be a proper woman. Foul language wasn't appropriate. Talking back wasn't appropriate. Being anything other than the submissive little house wife, always smiling and doing as she was told was the only thing that would ever be acceptable in this life.

It's a pity I wasn't like that. I had never been able to take it all lying down. I had been opinionated and strong from the start.

How could my parents have ever thought that this relationship with Reggie was a good match? How could they have believed that I would ever be happy?

Because it hadn't been about happiness. They had only been worried about my safety, I knew. My father hadn't told Reggie's parents that I would be a good wife because he believed I had something to offer that Reggie couldn't find in America. He had only thought about me being alive. And I understood that, in a way. I couldn't be angry with my father any more. I only missed him, now. I desperately wished we could go back to that time so I could see him again. So I could live in the house in London again.

How I missed home.

When I looked at Reggie again, I felt something inside me snap. For the past four months, I had bent over backwards to try make amends. I had done what I told him I would do—and I had been better. But this was what came of it. If this was all that was going to happen, what was the point?

"Well?" I asked him.

"Well what?"

"Are you going to say anything to your parents about how they treated me?"

Reggie pursed his lips together and I already knew what the answer would be before he said anything.

"I think we should discuss this after they leave," he said.

I knew what that meant. It was simply a diversion and we would never get around to actually discussing it. Not if he was the one that had to instigate the conversation. Reggie liked leaving things the way they were, and definitely preferred steering away from conflict. And if I was the one that brought it up again and initiated the conversation—even saying that he had told me we could speak about it—it would only end in a fight.

But I didn't say any of that. I didn't argue with him now. I just nodded curtly, plastered the damn smile on my face that everyone expected, and followed Reggie out of the kitchen.

We were going to make it through this day, I decided. We were going to be all smiles and good manners and try our best to please the in-laws. Not that it was ever possible.

But deep down, the resentment was starting to build again. For a while, I had truly believed that things could change. But the truth was, nothing had changed at all. People didn't change. My life with Reggie would always be the same. I would never be enough, and I would always feel incomplete. And there would always be this empty promise of a life where I would have been happy hanging over my head.

I had been an idiot to believe that things were going to change, that we might be able to move forward doing things differently than before.

I should have known that everything would stay the same. I should have known that Reggie was incapable of being a different man. And I guess, in a way, it was unfair of me to expect that of him, just as it was unfair of him to expect me to be someone different than who I was.

But after four months of sincerely trying, it was a slap in the face to know that it had all been for nothing.

What really got me every time, what swept my feet out from under me so that I fell so hard I couldn't catch my breath, was the belief that things would be different. When I had married Reggie, I had done so with the peace of mind that at least Junior and I would be safe. We would be cared for. I hadn't prepared myself for being unhappy. So then when I was unhappy, it had come as a shock.

Now, again, I had expected things to be different. And now that they weren't, it was like someone had thrown a bucket of ice water in my face. Again.

But, just like before, I would recover. I just didn't know how much longer I would be able to continue accepting us as we were.

Chapter 5

Thomas
Present Day

WHEN AMELIA ASKED ME if I wanted to see Claire again, I didn't know how to answer. Of course, I wanted to see my English girl again. It had been so long and I had only had her face in my dreams to keep me company.

But it was also a terrifying thought and I wasn't sure I had what it took. Because I had done everything in my power over the last few decades to forget the woman who had broken my heart. When I had gone back for her, traveled all the way to London to find her, she had been missing. At first, I thought that she might have been killed. London had been bombed again, several times, and so many lives had been lost. Despair and agony had riddled the faces of every person I had come across.

But I had learned from the only person on the property at the time I had reached her house—the mailman—that Claire had left London. And that she wouldn't be back.

That news had broken me and there had been no point in continuing to look for her. There had been no point in trying again.

And then, the only thing left had been to find a way to forget her.

But now, fifty years later, sitting here in the very same room I had sat every day, I was looking at two young faces who were offering me a chance to see her again.

Honestly, I was struggling to stay in the present. Since the moment they had mentioned Claire Whiteside's name, I had been transported back in time, back to London, to the gray streets and the upright manner of the people there, to the acrid smell of war in the air.

I rubbed my eyes with my thumb and forefinger, trying to separate the present from the past. My mind wasn't what it used to be. Since I had come back from the war, I had struggled with flashbacks and nightmares. And now, in my old age, I was struggling with my memory, too. Although, I would never forget her face.

"I don't know if I can do that," I finally said, looking at Amelia. She had patiently waited for me to answer. How much time had passed since she had asked the question?

"Why not?" She asked. Dane put his hand on her arm as if he wanted to stop her from prying too much or pushing too hard. What a dear boy. But I could see the questions on their faces, the intensity of what they were trying to do. And I understood it. I just didn't know if I had the energy to match their spirit.

"I don't think my heart will be able to handle it. It would only be a reminder of everything I lost. It's a whole lifetime, gone."

Amelia's face softened. She was such a sweet girl, so charming. Since the moment I had opened the door, I had liked her. I knew these things about people, knew what they were made of on the inside, not only how their actions defined them. And this was a good one. She leaned forward to me, her eyes full of hope, sitting on the edge of her seat. She reached for me, tentatively, as if she didn't want to scare me away. And when she touched my hand, her skin was warm and soft. It was a reassuring touch, something I hadn't felt in a very long time.

I looked down at our hands. She was so young, the skin on her hands smooth and free of liver spots. My hands were old, mangled, and scarred. But somehow, I didn't mind the contrast. And I didn't feel like she was invading my space and my life. I could feel my hands trembling in hers, and she only gently squeezed them, reassuring.

"Thomas, I know that this is terrifying. I can only imagine the kind of love that you two felt for each other, and to have lost that must have been the kind of heart ache that could kill you."

I nodded. That was correct. It was.

"Just because the two of you lost each other, doesn't mean you can't take steps to find each other again. It's not too late. You are both still alive and kicking, and there might just be something there. Maybe there is still love."

I didn't say anything.

"Maybe there isn't," she continued. She was realistic. I liked that about her, a dreamer, but with her feet on the ground. "Don't you think it would be better to know for sure rather than let an opportunity slip through your fingers?"

And that was where she had me. Because if I let Claire get away a second time, it would be on me. The first time, was unclear.

My hands started trembling more, but Amelia only held them tighter.

When I didn't answer for the longest time, she smiled at me.

"You can think about it," she said. "Dane and I are here until the day after tomorrow and then we're going back to Pinewood. I hope you will choose to come with us. I think Claire would be very happy to see you."

I nodded and she finally let go of my hands. Immediately, I wanted the warmth back, the reassurance when she held onto me. I hadn't realized how long I had felt so completely lost and alone.

"Okay," I said. "I'll think about it and I'll let you know before you leave."

Amelia and Dane looked at each other, something passing between them.

Looking at them, it was so easy to see how much they felt for each other. They didn't look comfortable around each other like they had known each other for a very long time, but they were definitely connected in a way that very few people experienced. They didn't know how lucky they were, how few people managed to find a connection like that in their entire lifetime, let alone so young. I hoped that they would continue to cultivate it, to make sure that they never last that connection. It was so important to fight for these things that were so very rare.

The conversation turned to other subjects and they did not leave right away. Instead, I offered them another cup of coffee, a few more biscuits. I wanted to offer them lunch, but I didn't have enough food in the house. I hadn't had company in months.

But neither of them seemed to mind. In fact, they were perfectly happy just making conversation. Small talk. I ended up telling them about the ranch, about what it was like living out here. And they were so interested, fascinated by my lifestyle, happy to hear about what I did here. I hadn't had someone interested in what I did for a living for a very long time, and talking about it reminded me of the passion I had for what I did. For the last couple of years, I'd only been going through the motions, doing what I needed to do because it would be a shame to let the family business die.

But I loved being a rancher. I loved living with so much space around me, and in speaking about it, that love was very quickly rekindled.

And I enjoyed their company so very much, I had half a mind to ask them to stay here with me until their visit ended.

But they needed to leave, and I needed the space to think. I needed to be able to get my mind straight, to get my head clear so I could make a decision about whether or not I was going to see Claire again. And I couldn't do that with the two people in my house who had brought my past crashing down on me again. No, I needed them to leave so that I could be alone, so that I could focus on what I needed to do.

Because right now, after Amelia had asked me the question about seeing Claire again, I hadn't been able to give her an answer.

A part of me wanted to see Claire so very badly, to hold her again, to touch her, to hear the sound of her beautiful voice.

But another part of me wanted nothing to do with the woman who had broken her promise, the woman who had left me behind, searching high and low for her only to realize that she had gone by choice.

"I think it's time we go," Dane said, and I was pulled back to the present. I wasn't sure if I had missed part of the conversation or if we had all sat in silence for a while. My mind betrayed me sometimes, taking me away to other places when I should have had manners and made conversation.

"Thank you so much for coming to see me," I said, when we all stood.

"We will see you again, soon," Amelia said, stepping forward to give me a hug. Dane shook my hand.

I walked them to the door. When they stepped out into the sun, they both commented on the beauty of the ranch again. And I looked at it through eyes that had never seen it before.

It really was a spectacular place. But I didn't like seeing it like this, through fresh eyes. Because it only reminded me of the promises I had made to Claire, the dreams we had woven together.

Dane and Amelia walked to the car they had arrived in and I watched as they climbed in, with Dane opening the passenger door for her before running over to the driver's side. It was good to know that chivalry was not yet dead. So many young people these days seem to forget what it was really about, how to court a lady, how to respect her and make her feel like she was special.

I really liked Dane and Amelia. I liked how they were with each other, how they spoke and the way they looked at each other. It reminded me of Claire, the way I used to look at her and speak to her. And the way she used to respond to me, and smile.

After watching the car until it disappeared around the bend, I turned toward the ranch house.

I had meant to spend the day working on the ranch, even though it was a Sunday and everyone else was resting. But now that Dane and Amelia had been here and dropped this bomb on me, I felt the need to rest. I was emotionally drained and just exhausted, so I needed to lie down. And I had so much to think about.

As I walked into the house, my mind was with Claire again.

But I didn't think about the prospect of seeing her again. I didn't try to decide if I was going to take Amelia up on her offer.

Instead, I saw Claire's dark eyes, her hair curled in perfect ringlets, and her blood red lips smiling at me.

Walking up to my bedroom, I lay down on the bed. Taking a deep breath, I closed my eyes and immediately was back in that bar in London. The music from the gramophone was floating around me, Claire's body was close to mine and her lips were close to my ear, whispering to me.

Chapter 6

Claire

I STOOD ON MY VERANDA, looking out over the stretch of land that I was now the sole owner of. When Reggie had died, the property in its entirety and the Rose Guild, had gone to me. I was a rich woman.

But I had never cared about the money, the title, the image, and everything else that had been so damned important to that man. I had cared about love and passion, and most of all, freedom.

None of which I had ever gotten.

But my life was mine own now. I could reclaim it. I could make it my own again. It had been fifty years, but I was the only one that had a say now.

And it was high time I exerted myself.

But how? I had nothing left to live for. Nothing worth my while. The girl I had once been, the girl with passions and dreams, with future plans and a lust for life that could not be matched by anyone, was gone. She had slowly faded away over the first decade of marriage to Reggie.

And a submissive, bitter woman had remained.

When I looked back at the person I used to be, I was saddened. I had been full of so much hope once, and joy. But it had been dampened by a man who had forced me into a mold.

I may not have known who I had become, who this woman was that was left in the wake of destruction now that Reggie was dead. But I knew that I could choose. For the first time in a long time, I started thinking ahead again. To a life without Reggie, without the person I should have been.

The garden looked terrible, if I had to be frank. I had ripped up all the rosebushes. Every single one of them. Dane had helped, the dear boy, but I hadn't allowed the gardening service to take care of it.

And it had felt good, getting rid of those damned roses that I had come to hate so much. The Whiteside Guild, Reggie had suggested I call it. In honor of my parents. What a lark. There was no honor, no pride. Reggie had only forced his dreams on me and hidden it behind good intentions and sympathy for what I had lost.

Well, that was over with now. I would dissolve the Guild and allow someone else in the county to step up and take over. I never wanted to see a rose in my life again.

My life was my own, now. Without those blasted bushes there was nothing to remind me of Reggie.

It was what I had wanted all along, though it had taken me far too long to get to this point. I turned my head toward the sun and closed my eyes, basking in the warmth. The season had turned and we were headed on toward fall now. Before long it would be winter and everyone would retreat indoors, and the snow would cover everything, suffocating the earth like a blanket.

I loved the snow the most and it reminded me of home. Soon, it would be here again. I couldn't smell it in the air, yet. But it was on its way.

Turning back toward the house, I needed a cup of tea and would have it here on the veranda where I could look out at the clean slate that was my life. This garden had become a metaphor, the very depiction of who I was. At first, the clean soil, just waiting to be cultivated, like when I had married Reggie and he had brought me home. And then the rose bushes that had been planted, young, filled with so much potential.

Throughout the years they had grown, struggled, and not been good enough. The very bane of my existence because they reflected me. And then, when they had finally taken off and the Guild had been established, becoming the face of Pinewood. Yet only I knew the pain that hid behind them.

It was so much of who I was, so much of who I had been.

And now, ripped out and dying in the dumpster. While I looked at the patches of dark earth where they had been ripped up, I saw the new life that could grow there instead.

Oh, the potential, the symbolism, the beauty.

Hearing a car pull up, I turned, hoping to see Dane. He hadn't been to visit the last few days and I'd missed his company. Since the shooting the poor boy had often been here and I had become so fond of him, more so than I had even been before.

But it wasn't Dane's truck in the driveway. Rather, it was Junior's Mercedes, the new, fancy model of his. The one that turned heads and screamed how much money he made doing whatever it was that he did now.

I sighed. Junior barely came to see me anymore. We had been so close, once upon a time. When he had been a little boy. But he had grown up, realized his mother was nothing but an old, sour woman, and he had moved on with his life, aspiring to be like Reggie instead.

I guess I deserved that, after everything I had done.

"Mother!" he said, coming up the steps to the veranda. "What happened to the garden?"

"I'm well, thank you, and you?" I asked sarcastically.

He rolled his eyes, a gesture Reggie had made so many times I had lost count. Reggie had always rolled his eyes at me. I wondered, had Junior known who his real father had been, would he have become so similar to Reggie? Or would he have become like Thomas? He still looked like the man I had once loved.

The dark eyes, the square jaw, the serious face. The height.

But the man I had once loved was nowhere else to be seen than in Junior's features. He was Reggie's child completely. Conceited, and solely concerned with his image.

I shouldn't have blamed him. I had been a sour, bitter woman for a very long time. I'd had terrible mood swings. During Junior's teenage years, I had done nothing but drive him away. It hadn't been intentional, not losing my son, too. But I had been such an awful person, so caught up in my own misery, I had been unable to see past my own pain.

Now, I could clearly see all the mistakes I had made. How I wished I could go back in time and change the way I had been, the things I had done. But they did say that hindsight is perfect sight. And I had to agree. If I had known then what I knew now, I would have done many things very differently.

But wasn't it always like that?

"So, what happened?" Junior asked, after stiffly kissing my cheek.

"I've always hated the roses, dear," I said.

"The Whiteside Guild. You hated it," Junior said incredulously. Making a sarcastic statement rather than asking a question.

I sighed. "I don't expect you to understand, darling. There are so many things I haven't allowed myself to feel for the longest time. But that stops now." I looked at Junior. He looked tired.

"How are you?" I asked. "How is work treating you?"

"It's going well at work," Junior said, skipping the first question. If I wanted him to answer every question, I needed to ask them one at a time. Junior didn't share his life with me anymore. The only reason he stopped by at all was because he felt obligated to check in on me from time to time. The last time he had really been here for a visit was before Reggie had passed away. When Junior had still felt he had something to say, something to come home to.

A pang of sadness shot into my chest. Junior had rejected me, even though I was his mother. And he had clung instead to the image Reggie had carried around, as if Reggie had been his father.

"Tea?" I offered.

Junior shook his head. "I'm not staying long."

Of course, he wasn't.

"Have you seen Dane lately?" Junior asked.

I nodded. "He comes by often. He's the one that helped me with the roses, actually. He's a good boy." I glanced at Junior. "I can't begin to tell you where he got that from."

Junior sighed. Of course, he would have no idea what I was referring to. He shook his head as if he had meant to say something and changed his mind. He looked at me, his dark eyes so like Thomas's that my heart nearly skipped a beat. But again, I was aware of how far the comparison went, and where it ended. Junior had grown up with Reggie as his father. He was Reggie's boy, through and through.

"Are you okay, though? With Dad gone? I mean, the roses..."

He looked out over the garden again, a look of longing on his face and I envied him. I envied him his ignorance, his affection for Reggie, the relationship they had shared. Reggie had always accepted Junior, but not me.

But that was all in the past. I shook it off. It was time to start living again. I had been dying for nearly fifty years.

"I'm perfectly fine," I said brightly. Maybe, it wasn't the complete truth. But I couldn't confide in Junior. Not about the things I felt, the things that haunted me, my past that seemed to come back more and more these days. Since that Amelia girl had arrived with that letter.

Junior wouldn't understand. How could he? There was so much of my life I had kept secret from him. So much I had done. All it would do if I confided in him about it now was ruin our relationship even more. And there was so little left of it to start off with.

"Well, I just came to see if you were alright, to check in," Junior finally said. There was so much between us that was left unsaid, so much hanging in the air that I felt sometimes like I would choke on it. Was this what happened to all relationships that died out? The same had happened with Reggie when he and I had drifted apart. And we hadn't even had a close relationship to begin with.

"Thank you for stopping by," I said, with the same forced smile. "Let me know when you are on your way next time, and I'll make us some lunch."

"I will," Junior said, even though we both knew that he wouldn't. He didn't want to spend a whole afternoon with me, didn't want to have lunch together. He always dropped by unannounced so that he could have a ready excuse to leave. He was always on his way to something else.

I watched him walk down the steps to the veranda, climbing back in his Mercedes, and backing out the drive. My heart was heavy as I watched my son go.

When exactly had I lost him? I wasn't sure. He had lived with me in the house all along, but one day, I had realized he was gone. He had withdrawn, and somehow gotten closer to Reggie than he was to me. It had been a tragedy. Junior had always been the only connection to Thomas I had left. But at some point, that had disappeared, too. Since then, I had been alone in my yearning—for something I had would never have.

But this feeling of loss and mourning and grief was an old one. We were great friends, these bitter emotions and I. And when Junior's car disappeared from view, I turned around and walked back to the house to put on a pot of tea and continue with my usual routine. There was no use losing time worrying over what could have been. I knew from experience that it didn't change anything.

Chapter 7

Dane

WHEN WE HAD MADE THE trip to Montana, we were focused on finding Thomas Brown. And we had done exactly that. It was crazy to think that we had managed to pull it off.

What we hadn't planned for was the trip turning into a romantic weekend away, getting closer to each other and spending quality time.

The bed-and-breakfast where we stayed was a quaint place, not nearly as extravagant as the ranch, but quite stunning in its own right. Being away from home, away from all the memories, thoughts and routines that we had there, Amelia and I could really focus on each other.

The older couple who ran the bed-and-breakfast were just wonderful people. We had met Ellen when we arrived, only meeting her husband Jacob the next morning when he offered the use of a car. We enjoyed breakfast with them every morning and it looked like they enjoyed our company, too. We had learned that during off peak season, they hardly had any visitors and were glad to have the company.

Now that we had found Thomas, Amelia and I were in a state of bliss. We sat at the large table in the kitchen, with Jacob and Ellen sitting with us, all of us enjoying freshly brewed coffee. I didn't know what it was, but everything tasted different out here. Better. Like an adventure.

"I think it's all just so romantic," Ellen said, after we had told our story. At first, Amelia and I hadn't shared what we were doing in Montana, but now that we had found Thomas, neither of us had been able to keep it a secret. Amelia had even gone to the bedroom and brought down the letter to show Ellen. She had read it with misty eyes.

It had turned out that Jacob and Ellen knew Thomas very well. Of course, Thomas Brown was a big name in the county, with one of the most famous ranches around. And the community in Stevensville wasn't a very large one. It was a lot like Pinewood and other small towns in the sense that everyone knew their neighbors business.

When I realized that Jacob and Ellen knew Thomas, I wondered if it had been a mistake to tell them what had happened, and that maybe we had told them secrets Thomas may have wanted to keep to himself.

But it was too late now, and thankfully, Jacob and Ellen didn't seem like the type of people that would spread gossip just for the sake of causing trouble. They were very warm people, caring and compassionate.

I was willing to believe that our story was safe with them.

"Can you even imagine if the two of them could be connected again after all this time?" Jacob said. "But my heart goes out to them. I couldn't imagine having lost Ellen so soon into our relationship, and then only connecting fifty years later."

I nodded. What had happened to my grandmother and Thomas was tragic, but the good news was that it didn't have to be the end of their story. They didn't have to die all alone, wondering what could have been. They could meet each other again, make up for lost time and still spend their final years together.

At least, that was how I saw it playing out in my mind. Of course, Thomas still had to decide that he was going to come back to Pinewood with us. And my grandmother would still have to decide that she wanted to see him. There were still so many uncertainties. But I was going to hold onto hope.

Look how far we had come. Against all odds, we had found Thomas. What else could happen?

"What about you?" Amelia asked. "How did you meet? How did your story start?"

I looked at Amelia, all the more drawn to her when she did things like this. She was sincerely interested in everyone's history and always made people so comfortable as they shared their stories with her. Everything with her was an adventure.

Ellen and Jacob looked at each other with so much love and adoration, it made my heart ache. To think that people could love each other so much.

Before I met Amelia, I had been certain that this kind of love was only for books and movies. It wasn't real, because in real life, people only got hurt. Sure, people were attracted to each other and lust was a big thing that may have brought some kind of connection. But I had never believed that a love existed that could transcend distance, time and the everyday trials of life.

Then I had met Amelia, and this story had come to light. What I had started feeling for her, combined with the revelation of what my gran and Thomas had felt for each other, made me question everything I had believed about love before.

And now, Ellen and Jacob were just another example that this kind of love might be real.

"Oh, ours is a very dull story, I'm afraid," Ellen said. "I was a secretary at the law firm my father had started. Jacob was one of the interns, recommended by the mother of a friend."

Jacob nodded. "I walked into those offices and promptly forgot why I was there. When I saw Ellen, my whole world changed."

Amelia listened to them with stars in her eyes. I watched her and couldn't help but think she was the most beautiful person I had ever seen. It was a little how I'd felt when she showed up in that yellow Volkswagen Beetle, pulling into my grandmother's driveway, having absolutely no right to be on private property.

She had swept my feet right out from under me. In more ways than one. Repeatedly.

"It didn't take very long before I knew that Ellen was the woman I wanted to spend the rest of my life with," Jacob said, continuing his story. "But she was playing hard to get," he chuckled. "Don't all women?"

Amelia and I glanced at each other, grinning.

Ellen laughed and reached out to Jacob, squeezing his hand.

"I just wanted to make sure you were worth the effort. To see if you were willing to fight for me."

Jacob pulled Ellen tightly against him. "I will fight day and night to make it work with you, my dear. You know that I would never have given up."

"And that's why you two are together," Amelia said, grinning. "It's so romantic."

Amelia smiled.

I watched her as she listened, enraptured, as Jacob and Ellen told their story. She was absolutely focused on all the things they were sharing with us. About their first date, the engagement, and the wedding. And I wondered, how did they know? How had they known that this was to be their story, and that it had begun? My grandmother and Thomas had a story, too. Had they known that it was starting when it had? Or had it crept up on them, and suddenly, they found themselves in the middle of something they had never expected?

When I looked at Amelia, I could imagine us being together for a long time. She was wonderful in every way.

Was this how it happened? Was this our story?

If it was, it was a beautiful way to start, I thought. I wasn't a romantic, I wasn't serious about history and had never really cared how poetic something sounded. But with Amelia, I was starting to look at everything differently. And wasn't that what it was all about? Wasn't part of being with someone the fact that they changed the way you looked at life?

Because Amelia had certainly changed the way I looked at mine. She had taught me how to move forward again after everything had fallen apart for me. I hadn't thought I would ever get past the shooting, or losing my partner and best friend, Drew. But now, with Amelia in my life, I found that I barely thought about the shooting anymore. I still had moments where anxiety got to me, and I still struggled with nightmares sometimes, but I had something else to look forward to, something else to occupy my thoughts and my time with.

Amelia was like a ray of light in my life, and I wanted more of that.

"So, what happens now?" Ellen asked, and I realized they were back on the topic of Thomas and my grandmother.

"Well, we asked Thomas to come back to Pinewood with us," Amelia said. "I just worry that he might not want to."

Jacob nodded. "I could understand that. This is difficult. He has been a lonely man for a very long time."

Thomas had mentioned that his family had moved away a while ago and that he had been alone on the ranch for a while now. But hearing from Jacob that Thomas was alone somehow made it all seem so much sadder. My gran wasn't the only one who had lived a loveless life. She wasn't the only one who hadn't gotten what she deserved.

Thomas had suffered for a very long time, too.

"But if he does go," Ellen said, "it will finally be the closure he needs, and the answers he may have been asking himself for decades. I can't imagine what it must have been like for him to live with so many questions for so long."

We sat in silence for a while. At first, I thought about my gran and Thomas, and how unfair their love story was. But my thoughts drifted to Amelia. I wasn't going to let her slip through my fingers. I wasn't going to let anything get in the way of what could be between us. Of course, we didn't have a war raging around us, and that made everything easier.

But every relationship had obstacles, and I was willing to overcome them with her.

I felt a pang when I realized I referred to this thing between us as a relationship. But what else? After all, I wasn't aiming for a platonic friendship with her.

Reaching for her, I was running my hand down her arm, and even though she didn't look at me, when my hand reached hers she intertwined our fingers.

I loved how she responded to me, how she made me feel like even when she was doing something else, I was still at the forefront of her mind.

She was on my mind and I wanted to be alone with her now.

I squeezed her hand and when she glanced at me, I lowered my voice a little. "Are you ready to head back up and get ready for bed?"

Her face lit up, her smile widening and she was stunning. It was as if I was seeing some things about her for the first time. She had a smattering of freckles on her nose and cheekbones that I hadn't seen before. Was it because she always wore make up? Her hair curled a little, as if the change in climate had affected it somehow, and what I saw now was a raw, natural beauty shining through that I somehow hadn't noticed before. How was that even possible?

But all this time, we had been focusing on the love story, careful around each other because of how comfortable it felt. Because it was too good to be true, wasn't it?

But no, Amelia really was as great as she had been from the start, and nothing was going to change. It wasn't too good to be true. I was just extremely lucky.

Amelia and I ended our conversation with Ellen and Jacob and bade them good night. With our fingers still intertwined, we left the kitchen and walked to our bedroom. I followed Amelia, and as I walked behind her, I realized this was it. This was where everything changed for us. Not because we were going to do anything different, not because anything had changed at all.

But because I was falling hopelessly and desperately in love with her.

Chapter 8

Amelia

I HAD BEEN IN RELATIONSHIPS before, but nothing had ever felt anything like this. Nothing had felt the way it felt with Dane. We were connected on a level I had never experienced with anyone. When I gave myself to him, something that had happened very naturally with him, I knew that he would take care of me. He wasn't going to hurt me.

When I fell for him, Dane would catch me.

When he had suggested we head for our room, I had known what he wanted. I didn't even care that Ellen and Jacob probably knew, too. After all, they were in love, and they couldn't possibly have missed what Dane and I felt for each other. Besides, after talking about meeting your soul mate for so long, romance was thick in the air.

So we locked ourselves in our room and Dane pulled me closer to him, so close that a sigh would press us together.

"I'm so glad I'm here with you," he said. His face was only inches away and I could smell the wine we had been drinking on his breath. It mingled with my own and his closeness made my heart beat faster.

"I'm so glad to be with you, too," I said softly.

Dane kissed me and I melted against him. His tongue slid into my mouth and I moaned softly. I touched him, my hand on his inner thigh and I slowly ran it upward. Dane made a growling sound at the back of his throat. The lust was suddenly so thick between us it became difficult to breathe. But it wasn't only lust. There was so much affection as well. Being with Dane just felt right.

And I knew that I wasn't the only one feeling it.

Dane wrapped his arms around me and walked me to the bed, our lips still fused together, our bodies pressed tightly against each other. When we reached the bed, he tugged me down and we collapsed on the mattress, facing each other. He kissed me again and I loved the feel of his lips on mine, the coarseness of this stubbled chin scraping against me. His tongue slid into my mouth again and I moaned softly.

After a moment, Dane rolled on top of me and he kissed me harder. I felt the erection in his pants. He ground his hips against me. I ran my hands down his back and found the bottom of his shirt. I pushed my hands under it, palms on his bare skin for a while, while we made out.

But I wanted more. I wanted him naked.

I pulled the shirt up and he lifted a little, and helped me work it over his head. When the shirt was off, I threw it on the ground next to the bed.

Dane moved off me, sitting up, and he pulled off my shirt, too. He leaned forward and kissed me on the neck, the scrape of his stubble giving me goosebumps, while he reached around me and unclasped my bra. His hands found my breasts and he massaged them, softly tweaking my nipples. I moaned into his mouth.

Suddenly, he moved off me and started undoing his belt. It was as if he had gotten irritated with wearing pants. I smiled at him while he undressed himself. He stood in front of me, naked, and his erect cock stood up proudly. But it wasn't his spectacular body that drew my attention, or the way he was clearly ready to take me. It was the way he looked at me.

His eyes were dark, drowning deep. The look on his face was intense, but it wasn't only lust that I saw. His features were riddled with affection and adoration, and for some reason, a lump rose in my throat.

I never had a man look at me the way Dane was looking at me now. Especially not while we were headed toward having sex. But he looked at me as if I was the only thing he wanted in this world, the only person he would ever care for.

"Have I told you how beautiful you are?" he asked. And I knew he wasn't saying it because I sat topless in front of him.

I couldn't help myself and blushed furiously.

Dane climbed onto the bed again, moving slowly, his eyes on mine. He kissed me again, pushing me backward so I lay down again, and while he kissed me, he fiddled with my own jeans.

I helped him undo them, but he peeled them off me, over my hips and then down my legs. He sat back and pulled them off, one leg after the other.

And then we were both naked.

Dane ran his hands up and down my legs, his eye roaming my body. He looked at me with the same affection, his hands following the contours of my body.

Slowly, he made his way closer and closer to my pussy and I shivered, trembling with need.

When Dane pushed his fingers into me, I moaned.

"You're so wet for me," he whispered.

I nodded, biting my lip, watching him as he lowered his face between my legs.

When he licked my clit I cried out. He sucked on me, making my quiver, and his fingers were still inside of me. He stroked them slowly in and out as he sucked on my clit and I was certain I was going to lose my mind.

The orgasm built slowly as he licked me and fucked me with his fingers and I curled and squirmed on the bed, moaning and gasping.

Before I could orgasm, he let go.

"Don't stop," I gasped in a breathy voice.

"Not yet, baby," Dane said, and my stomach flipped when he called me that. He kissed me and I could taste myself on him. And it was delicious.

"Let me return the favor," I said.

Dane shook his head. "Nope. Tonight is all about you."

He kissed me again before I could argue. He was so caring and attentive, and even though we were about to have sex, he made me feel like this was all about me, and who I was as a person, not just about my body.

As we made out, his hands roamed my body again. I wanted him so badly, the orgasm he'd built having subsided again a little and I desperately wanted a release.

I reached for him and he lifted his body a little so I could wrap my fingers around his dick. He groaned when I did and kissed me harder.

When he shifted again, I opened my thighs for him and he positioned himself between them, pressing the head of his cock against my entrance. I held my breath in anticipation and moaned when he slid into me, slowly, caressingly. When he was buried all the way, he stayed there without moving. I trembled lightly around him. Dane's eyes were locked on mine again. He ran his fingers through my hair and the feeling that grew between us was so much more than lust.

This wasn't fucking. This was making love.

Dane started moving inside me and I moaned when he did. He moved slowly at first, stroking in and out, allowing me to feel every inch of him. I closed my eyes and focused on how he felt inside of me, the weight of his body on mine. He kissed me again and I lost myself in him.

Dane started picking up pace and I moaned louder, panting in rhythm with his sex. Warmth spread through my body, the heat building as the tension he had built earlier returned with a vengeance. When he pumped harder and harder, I toppled over the edge into an orgasm and my body tightened around his. Dane chuckled and when I opened my eyes and looked at him, he looked at me with so much affection. I was drowning in how much seemed to care for me.

"I love it when you do that," he said.

"What?"

"Come for me. Because of me."

I didn't have time to blush about how blunt he was being. He started bucking his hips again, moving faster and faster. I moaned and cried out, trying to keep it down so that we didn't scare the poor old people. But we all knew what was happening here tonight.

Dane stopped and I moaned, unhappy. I wanted more. He slipped out of me. I didn't know what he had in mind, but I knew what I wanted. I took control, nudging him so that he lay on his back, and I climbed onto him. I sunk onto his dick and we both groaned when I did. Slowly, I started riding him, moving faster and faster as he had. He reached up for my breasts while I bucked my hips back and forth, his face riddled with lust and pleasure.

I didn't orgasm, and I didn't make him come, either. Instead, after a while, I climbed off of him.

Dane sat up, pulling me closer to him, and kissed me. I kissed him back before I turned around. He knew what I wanted, and I loved how he moved, positioning himself behind me, putting his hands on my hips.

He pushed into me and I cried out. I braced myself on the mattress, hands curling around the blankets as he pumped into me from behind. I tried my best not to cry out too loudly, but he was stroking my G-spot and another orgasm was approaching hard and fast.

And judging by the way he gasped, the speed of his strokes and the way he gripped my hips, he was getting closer, too.

We were both lost in sexual bliss as he hammered into me. Dane reached deeper into me than ever before and I cried out as I climaxed first. Not long after, Dane thrust himself into me and I felt him jerking inside me as he released. We orgasmed together, as we had before, and even though we weren't facing each other, I was still so aware of our connection, of everything between us that seemed to be getting stronger and stronger no matter what we did.

It felt like our orgasms continued forever. Finally we came down from the high and Dane pulled out of me. He was still semi-erect, but he pulled me against him and we lay down on the pillows together. The sheets were a tangled mess. We would fix that, later.

I didn't know what it was about Dane. No matter what we did sexually, no matter how intense or dirty or seemingly driven by lust things got, it was always about the two of us. It was never just about sex.

And I loved that about him. I loved a lot of things about him.

How had this happened? How had I gotten involved with a man that was so decent, so wonderful to me? Who got this lucky?

Well, the answer was obvious. Me. But I had never expected something like this to happen. I had never thought that I would fall in love. I had moved away from the city to change my life, and I had. But this was a curve ball I hadn't expected.

Still, I couldn't be happier. Here with Dane, the world was right. Nothing else mattered. If Thomas decided to come with us, that would be great. If he didn't, that was okay, too. I had been so hung up on a happy ending I missed the fact that I'd already found it.

I just hadn't realized it was my own.

"Are you okay?" Dane asked, tightening his arm around me.

"More than okay," I said. I looked up at Dane and he kissed me on the forehead.

"Good," Dane said. "Me too."

I smiled and curled tighter against Dane. He squeezed me with his arm and I closed my eyes, smiling. How happy could one woman be?

Infinitely.

Chapter 9

Claire
1956

I HAD STOPPED HOPING for better times because then when it went worse instead, it was a slap in the face. I thought it would prepare me for the rest of my life, that if I didn't keep hoping, I couldn't get hurt.

But I was wrong. Things still got worse. And it still felt like an absolute betrayal. Betrayed by who? I didn't even know anymore. I just knew that this was not what happiness was supposed to look like. I knew that this was not what a happy ending sounded like.

Somehow, even though Reggie and I had told each other that we would try to do better, and change things between us, it had only gotten worse again.

Not worse than it had been in April, with Easter, but worse than it had been, ever.

It wasn't that Reggie hurt me. Not physically—he would never do that. Reggie was a lot of things, but he was not an abusive husband. No, it was other things.

He ignored me. It was like I didn't exist. I was this invisible being that cooked and cleaned and organized the house and did everything that I should do, and he didn't even know I was here anymore. It was like he didn't have a wife.

We were two people sharing a house, but we weren't living in it together. We hadn't for months now. Almost a year, in fact. When I cooked, we didn't eat together. Most of the time, Reggie sat in front of the television. That blasted invention should never have been created. I was sure that my husband wasn't the only one in the world that allowed it to take precedence over his family.

When Reggie ate in front of the television, I ate with Junior. Unless, of course, he was out with his friends. These days, it's all he seemed to be doing. He was easily away from home four or five times a week. I didn't blame him. If I could choose, I would be out of the house all the time, too.

There was no way that this was what family life looked like. And I knew that Junior felt the loss of what should have been, just as I did. Not in the same way, since he had never had a dream of happiness the same way I had. But surely, his friends had families and they spent time together in a different way than we did. Especially the ones he spent all his time at.

It made me bitter with jealousy. Why did other people have the right to my sons presence and I did not? And that only made me hate Reggie more, because it was because of him. If he would only spend time with us, if he would only care about us, maybe things would be different.

If I hadn't married him at all, things would have been different.

But that only yanked me back to the past. Because what other choice did I have? My father had promised me to Reggie, but I had been the one to ultimately not fight it. Because it had been safe. Because there had been promise of life, not death and fear. It was a way for Junior to be safe. That was all I had been thinking about.

I should have tried to imagine the future, to take everything into account. But I had been driven by fear and by my father's insistence. And here I was.

Walking into the living room, I switched off the lights. It was late, after ten already. Reggie was passed out on the sofa, surrounded by empty beer bottles. It seemed like he was always drinking, these days. He didn't even hide it anymore, not at home, anyway. To the public, he was still the upstanding gentlemen that lived in this household, but I knew better.

When I looked at him, I felt nothing but disgust. He was overweight, unbecoming, and a drunk.

I walked out of the large living room again, not even trying to wake him up. He would sleep here for the night.

Junior was out with friends. It was just me. And I was so incredibly alone.

I felt an ache in my chest. I rubbed my sternum with my fingertips, my mind wandering to Thomas. It was the first time I had thought about him in months. When Reggie and I had promised each other we would try, I had pushed Thomas from my thoughts completely. It had only been fair that I try to make things better if Reggie did, and I couldn't do that if I was actively still in love with another man.

But my love for Thomas would never die out. No matter how hard I tried. And now that my life had fallen apart again, thinking about him stirred a burning inside me that was terrifying.

What would my life have been if I had been with him? Would I feel this crippling loneliness?

All I needed was for someone to love me properly. I needed someone to see me for who I was, to touch me, to make me feel like I was alive again. Here, in this house, doing everything in my power to be noticed, yet failing despite it all, I was just dying away.

I walked to the bedroom and shrugged on a coat, checking my hair in the mirror. This reminded me so much of when I had snuck out to go to the bar where I had met Thomas. Because I was sneaking out now. I was going to town, to find someone to have a drink with. Or, if I was lucky, something more.

While I stood in the bedroom, looking at myself in the mirror, I was transported back in time. I was seventeen again, a young girl at the beginning of her life. I was brimming with excitement, glad to get out when I had been stifled by the war and my father trying to keep me away from the world. When I looked in the mirror now, I looked like a sad reflection of the girl I had once been. I still had the same face, albeit a lot more worn, a little older, a little less beautiful. My figure was roughly the same, too. Unlike Reggie, I had not let myself go. But time had taken its toll on my body just as it had on my face, and despite being upright, I could almost see how misery aimed at my shoulders, trying to drag me down.

That night, when I met Thomas, had been one of the most magical nights of my life. And my friends—oh, how I missed them. Nostalgia was thick in the air as I thought about Ruth, Margaret and Dorothy, the girls I had never seen again. I didn't even know if they were alive. I hadn't had contact with any of them since I left England.

Back then, my life had been fraught with danger. Not only because I had been a teenager, sneaking out and breaking rules, but because of the raging war. No one had known how long their life would last, or if we would even get through it at all.

But somehow, this seemed so much worse. The war had been terrifying, but there had been some kind of end in sight. Maybe not immediately, but we had all known that eventually, it would end.

I didn't feel like that now. I didn't feel like this terrible time in my life would end. It only stretched into infinity, with a terrible husband. There was no way out of this horrible life. I couldn't even jump on a plane and escape it. Not the way I had when my parents had sent me to America with Reggie and his tiresome parents.

Because this was my life now, this was my reality. There was nothing I could do about where I had ended up.

I shook off the thoughts of the past. Looking back, reminiscing about the time I used to be happy, wasn't going to change anything. It would only make me more miserable. And I was already in such a bad emotional space, if I made it worse for myself, who knew what I was going to do? I was already on my way to do something I had never really thought I was capable of. But loneliness, sadness and bitterness drove everyone to lengths that had once seemed impossible.

I left the house feeling incredibly guilty, but what else was I supposed to do? I needed someone to touch me. I needed human connection. I felt like I had been completely isolated, with only Reggie's family to gossip with and my cheeks were tired of faking smiles.

Somehow I needed to feel like a woman again. Reggie hadn't slept in our bed in weeks, months even. Let alone touch me. I needed more.

I took a cab to the bar, not willing to drive myself, and stood outside. I braced myself against the cold night air. It sliced through my coat despite being bundled up, and the few people walking past, either heading toward the bar or on their way somewhere else, had their shoulders hunched against the cold, and their heads tacked against the wind.

Winter was on the way, and fast. And I was out here in the middle of town at an ungodly hour, about to do things I definitely shouldn't.

For a moment, I was terrified of what I was about to do. Why was I here? What was I thinking? It would be better if I just went home. I lifted my hand to hail another cab.

I didn't know who would spend time at the pub at this time of night, and which of the people in there would know me. And even though I was increasingly unhappy, I still had image to uphold. Not to mention that Reggie would be furious if he found out I had been here, especially if he heard it from someone else who was happy to carry gossip.

But Reggie was a lot more well-known that I was in Pinewood, and I had a feeling that very few people remembered me. I didn't come out of the house very often and when I did, I barely spoke to anyone. I had been isolated for so long, no one would really know who I was anymore.

Before, that would have upset me. In London, everyone had known whose daughter I was, which house I belonged in.

But right now, maybe anonymity was a blessing. It would mean that I didn't have to worry about my actions. For the first time in a long time, if no one knew who I was, I would just be able to live for a change.

Finally, a cab approached. This was where I could go home.

But I decided against it and dropped my hand again. Reggie was at home, drunk, and passed out. Junior would come home tomorrow, or maybe the next day. I would sleep alone in the giant bed, wake up in the morning to complete the routine again. Nothing was going to change. Nothing was going to be different. The only thing that was going to happen was I was going to lose every single part of me that I was still fiercely clinging to.

No, I needed this. And I didn't have any other options. I wasn't going to survive if I didn't find some way to make me feel something. I turned and walked away from the road, heading toward the door of the bar, where golden light spilled out onto the curb, and laughter and music invited me in.

As soon as I was inside, I took a deep breath, smelling the tang of smoke in the air. It reminded me of Thomas. He had always smelled of smoke. I looked around, wondering how I had ended up in a place like this again, so many years later.

Chapter 10

Thomas
Present Day

THAT AMELIA GIRL HAD told me that she would be in town with Dane for another two days. That was how much time I had to think about going back to Pinewood to see Claire.

But I didn't think that all the time in the world would be enough for me to be able to decide. It had been decades since I had seen Claire. The last time I'd seen her I had been in Romford, recovering from an injury. She had found me, somehow, and we had shared with each other that we were each terrified our promises to each other didn't stand any more. We had renewed them, and told each other that we would always try to find each other after the war, then we would belong to each other once and for all.

And then? I had been shipped back out to the field because my injury hadn't been enough to send me home. Oh, if only it had. They were a lot of days where I imagined what it would have been like for me, had my injuries been bad enough to prevent my return to war.

Claire would have been able to stay by my side and I would have left for America soon after. And she would have come with me. We would have had the life we had dreamed of.

But no, I had gone back to battle. And because I had disappeared, so had Claire.

How was it possible that she could just forget about me like that? How could she marry someone else? The young people had told me that she hadn't loved him and had been forced into it. And after what she had told me about her father, that was something I could believe.

But I still felt abandoned. I had felt abandoned for all these years. It was only now that I had found out the truth, and I had strengthened myself against what I believed Claire had done to me.

And yet, I was in the bedroom now, staring at my packed suitcase. It was open on the bed and I had no idea if I was forgetting something.

How had this happened? I had told myself over and over again that going to see her was a mistake. Told myself that I would send the kids packing if they came knocking on my door again to check if I wanted to go along with them.

But I had taken the suitcase out from underneath my bed and started folding clothes, packing them neatly for the flight to Oklahoma. Because no matter how much I tried to stop myself, I couldn't stay away from Claire. My beautiful Claire. I had never been able to forget her and what we had shared.

During the last two days, I had told myself every reason I shouldn't go. She had married someone else. She didn't want to see me. She had forgotten who I was. The ranch needed me. I was the only one running it. I could run through a myriad of other reasons why going was a bad idea. And yet, here I was, ready to leave. Ready to jump again, even if it meant that I would be shattered as I had been before.

How much worse would it be to recover if Claire rejected me this time? It had taken me years to get over her, and even then, I hadn't truly gotten over her. I had just been able to live with the pain of not having her. I didn't think I would ever stop loving Claire and I would never be able to say that I had moved on.

What if she didn't want me now? What if it was the same as before?

I had never heard of the town called Pinewood. Then again, I had grown up in Montana, this was my home and there hadn't been a reason to travel far outside it. But now, I was going to take this wild leap and go somewhere I didn't know, all for my Claire.

My thoughts drifted to what she had looked like that first time I met her. She had been breathtakingly beautiful. And every time I had seen her, she had been even more so.

I wondered what she looked like, now. Was she still the same? I imagined she was old, gray and wrinkled, just like me. But surely, at her core, she still had to be the same woman.

Would she recognize me if she saw me, standing at her door? Would she wish that I had never come to find her again? Or would she be happy to see me?

Would she still love me? That was the biggest question, wasn't it?

All these questions were driving me crazy. It was one of the biggest reasons I had decided to go to Pinewood, even though a voice in the back of my mind was screaming at me that it was a bad idea. Because I couldn't live however many years I have left with all these questions unanswered. I had struggled for so long already.

Even if it hurts, finding the answers to all these questions would give me a measure of peace, at least. And a man of my age, with so many experiences behind him, deserved at least that.

I zipped up my bag and hoisted it off the bed, struggling to carry it to the front room. I wasn't the man I had once been and my strength was waning. I didn't know how long I had left, but it was now or never. And I wasn't the kind of man to cling to 'never' instead of pursing the 'now.'

Sitting down on the couch, I rubbed my palms on my knees, wondering how the hell I was going to be able to get through this.

Finally, a knock sounded at the door. I stood up and walked toward the door, pulling it open. Dane and Amelia stood in front of me, their faces bright.

I was so aware of their youth, their will and excitement for life. I had looked like that, once upon a time.

"Hello, Thomas," Amelia said, and she gave me a hug. Dane shook my hand. "How are you doing today, sir?"

"I'm all right," I said. "Do you want to come in?"

They nodded and I stepped aside, inviting them into my house for the second time this week. As soon as they were in the living room, Amelia looked down at the suitcase and she looked up at me with surprised eyes, a smile growing.

"Thomas, have you decided to come with us to Pinewood?"

I nodded slowly. "I think it's a terrible idea."

"Oh, no! I think it's a wonderful idea. I am so glad."

She was positively brimming with excitement and it was beautiful to see someone that was still capable of such intense feeling. Dane watched her with adoration and I could see that he believed her excitement was as beautiful as I did. Perhaps even more.

I had looked at Claire the way he looked at Amelia. He really loved her. I didn't quite know if Amelia was aware of it, but Dane would never see another woman again. Amelia would be the only person that existed to him.

When Amelia looked at him, I knew that she knew. And she felt the same. She reached for his hand and squeezed it, something passing between them, and it made me downright emotional. For two people to be aware of their affection for each other was one thing, but acting on it was entirely another. Amelia and Dane had found something very rare, and they seemed to be aware of it. And they were embracing it.

I wanted to tell them to never let it go, but it wasn't my place. And after this story, where they had found Claire Whiteside and eventually found me, I was almost sure that they already knew it anyway.

"I have to admit, I am scared out of my mind," I said.

Amelia's face softened and she stepped toward me, taking both my hands in hers just as she had done before. She was quite a bit shorter than I was. In fact, she was about as tall as Claire had been when I had met her.

"I know this is scary," she said. "But we will be there every step of the way. We'll catch you if you fall, and we will celebrate with you in your happiness."

She was such a darling girl. I could see why Dane was so fond of her.

"This is the right choice, Thomas," Amelia added. "No matter how this goes, you will no longer need to wonder."

And that was it, wasn't it? I would finally know for sure. Again, it was the promise of peace that really convinced me.

But no matter which way I painted it, no matter how I looked at it, this was still a terrifying thing to do. Not only was I going to leave my home to go after a girl that had abandoned me, when I had needed her the most in my mind. I was also going to travel again, to leave my home. I hadn't left the ranch since I had returned from the war. Not to visit my nieces in the city, not to go on a holiday, not to do anything. I had been too terrified that if I left here, I would never be able to come back again.

Returning from the war had been a miraculous feat that I had once thought I would never be able to manage. I had nearly died out there, more than once. I had nearly not come home at all.

But this? This was different. I wasn't heading out there to fight. I wasn't going away to sacrifice my life. And maybe, just maybe, I would gain something. The honest truth was that I wouldn't lose anything, not again. Because I didn't have anything left to lose this time. So, even if this went terribly wrong, I would just be right back where I started.

Except, I would be two friends richer. I already was. When Amelia told me that they would catch me when I fell, I believed her.

Travelling with Amelia and Dane would also mean that I could see more of the relationship growing between them, and the way that they were with each other. And seeing something like that, the warmth and affection, was something beautiful to behold. It would be a treat.

"How much time do we have left?" I asked. "Do we have time for a cup of coffee?"

Dane shook his head. "I'm afraid we have to get going to the airport. But we can have coffee there, after we checked in our luggage."

I nodded. Dane had his head screwed on right. The young man picked up my suitcase for me and started toward the door, opening it and letting me and Amelia walk-through. He loaded my suitcase into the trunk while Amelia opened the door for me and helped me into the car.

I hated being an old man. I hated needing other people to help me. But this was what my life had become, wasn't it? We all expire at some point.

Dane and Amelia sat in the front while I was in the back. As soon as Dane pulled off, I looked out the window, watching my ranch shrink as we drove away. It made my heart ache.

"You're coming right back again, Thomas," Amelia said, as if she knew what I was thinking. "But first, there is an adventure to be had."

Chapter 11

Dane

IF I HAD TO BE HONEST, I'd half expected Thomas to decline our request to come back to Pinewood with us. Of course, I was thrilled that he had decided to come—that had been the point of our little trip to Montana, after all—but he had seemed reluctant to leave his ranch. And I understood it, too. I had experienced something similar with my grandmother. It seemed that older people were less inclined to let go of the things they knew, their worlds gradually becoming smaller and smaller.

I had been worried that it would be a terrible disappointment to Amelia if Thomas told us he wasn't going to come with us. But now that he had agreed, Amelia was more excited than ever. I had to admit that I was very excited, too. Excited, and nervous.

Nervous, because I still wasn't sure how my grandmother was going to respond to this whole endeavor. After all, we hadn't told her what our plans were because I'd been sure she would have told me straight away not to bother coming to Montana at all. But my grandmother had become very negative and very bitter, and after everything she had told me about her past and her loveless life, I understood why.

I knew that I might be crossing a line by inviting Thomas to Pinewood without my grandmother's knowledge. But she deserved this. She deserved a happy ending now, more than ever. And so did Thomas. They had found true love at a very young age and the war and everything else had ripped it away from them. They deserved to get it back again, even if it was fifty years down the line.

As we drove to the airport, I glanced in the rearview mirror every now and then. Thomas sat in the back seat, looking out the window at the countryside sliding by. I was so thankful that Ellen and Jacob had loaned us the car. A cab would have been awkward for this trip and harder on Thomas. They had insisted, which was really sweet, saying they could easily pick it up later. I had been sure to leave a nice tip in the room for use of the car and the great hospitality, since they had refused me when I tried to pay them for it.

Having just the three of us in the car without a cab driver to contend with, just made it all more comfortable. Thomas was already doing so much, stepping out of his comfort zone completely, so I wanted to make things as smooth as possible for him.

Because even now, as comfortable as Thomas seemed to be with Amelia, the old man still looked very nervous. I couldn't blame him for that, either. This was a terrifying thing to do for him, and I completely understood that.

I wanted to tell him again and again that it was going to be alright. But honestly, I wasn't a hundred percent sure that it would be. What if my grandmother was mean to him? What if she turned him away without even wanting to look at him? Or what if they didn't hit it off, what if they fought?

No, I wasn't going to think that way.

As if Amelia sensed that my mind was going in a negative direction, she reached for my hand and squeezed it. When I glanced at her, her green eyes were bright and reassuring.

When we arrived at the airport, it was a case of going through the motions. Amelia and Thomas got out of the car and she escorted him into the airport while I ~~took~~ parked the car. When I headed into the airport building, I got a text from Amelia telling me where they were.

Together, we checked in ~~our~~ and headed toward the waiting lounge.

Amelia chatted the whole way, prattling on about this and that, and her sweet voice was nice to listen to. But I noticed that Thomas was shutting down more and more and I was a little worried about him. This was a daunting trip for anyone his age, let alone the added pressure of what we were going to do.

"Are you alright?" I asked, when Amelia disappeared to buy us all coffee.

Thomas nodded. He didn't say anything.

"Amelia and I will be at your side every step of the way," I said.

Thomas looked at me, his dark eyes boring into mine. "I know. You kids have been nothing but kind to me from the start. I really appreciate it."

I nodded, and we sat together in amicable silence. Amelia returned with the coffee and she started talking again, telling Thomas how beautiful Pinewood was.

"I only moved there a couple of months ago," she said. "But it's the kind of place you fall completely in love with. I don't think I'll ever leave again." As she stated that, she glanced at me and I smiled at her. I liked to think that Amelia wasn't going to leave again, not only because of how amazing Pinewood was, but because of what was happening between us. Because it was something serious, something bigger than I had ever thought possible with a woman.

Finally, the boarding call sounded and we stood, walking toward the gate. Amelia walked first, with Thomas following her, and I was behind him.

As soon as we headed toward the plane, Thomas looked like he was panicking. His steps faltered and his hands were trembling.

Suddenly, it dawned on me that his reaction might not be all about meeting my gran at all. Thomas had been through so much, so the plane could be triggering his reaction. And if anyone understood trauma, and how it could haunt you, it was me.

I stepped up beside Thomas. "I'm right here, Thomas," I said. "Every step of the way."

Thomas looked at me, let out a shuddering breath, and we took the next steps together.

Inside the plane, I arranged it so that I sat in the middle between Thomas and Amelia. I wanted to talk to Thomas, to see if I could help him and find out what was really going on. Amelia sat on my other side, fiddling with the headphones and I let her be. It was as if she understood that we needed a more private conversation.

"What's wrong, Thomas?" I asked.

He swallowed twice like he was really struggling.

"This is terrifying," he admitted.

"It's not because we're going to Pinewood, is it?"

Thomas shook his head. "No. This is the first time I've been on a plane since I came back home from the war."

I nodded, suddenly realizing what this was all about. I had recognized it as a response having something to do with trauma, but I had no idea quite how serious it was.

"I just don't like being in small spaces or crowds, I feel out of my depth. I can't keep track of everything around me, I can't tell when something is going to go wrong."

"Actually, I know how you feel to a degree," Dane said. "I've had my own run in with trauma and it's very difficult to deal with. But I can tell you this, you are a brave man for doing this at all. I think I might have backed down."

Thomas let out a breathy chuckle. He was obviously very nervous.

"It's ridiculous, really. I didn't even have anything to do with planes during the war. I was a foot soldier. But still, the idea of being in a plane again just scares me. I don't know what it is. Planes shouldn't remind me of the war at all."

"Maybe it's got to do with the fact that being on a plane was your escape from the horrors of war that you endured."

Thomas pulled up his shoulders. Scrubbed his face with one hand and he looked so much older for a moment, dragged down by the memories of his past. I knew all too well how that felt.

"Maybe," Thomas finally said. He looked around him, jolting anxiously when an air hostess appeared at his elbow to check the overhead compartments.

"It's going to be okay, Thomas," I said, even though I knew that reassuring words like that didn't really help very much. Everyone kept saying things were going to be okay for me too, and I knew how little difference it really made. But I was going to be here for Thomas. I was going to help him through this because I understood what it meant to irrationally fear everything around you.

"You know, when I got on a plane for the first time it was to go to London," Thomas said. "I had never been on a plane before and it was so damn exciting, then. Strange how things change, isn't it?"

No wonder. It made perfect sense why planes scared Thomas. If planes had delivered him to the place where he had suffered greatly, it only made sense that there were connections in his mind.

"Until then, I had only ever been here on the ranch, doing what was expected of me, growing up a real cowboy." He chuckled bitterly. "Oh, how war changed everything."

I nodded, sympathetic, but not knowing what to say. I might have been through my own trauma, but I hadn't been to war and I knew that it wasn't nearly the same. What I had experienced was nothing compared to what Thomas must have been through.

"I can't believe I was excited about going to London at all," Thomas said, deep in thought. I knew that he was back there, his mind back in time, the visions of the past before his eyes instead of everything around him." Seeing something new was great, but I should have known what it would mean. I should have known I would lose everything."

I knew that he wasn't talking about my grandmother when he said he had lost everything. War was different.

"It's strange, knowing that all the friends you make when you're going off to war might die all around you. Of course, being young and invincible, we didn't believe it would happen to us. We heard all the stories about everyone else and were determined to be different, to come back as heroes. But it doesn't take very long on the battlefield, seeing the blood flow and tasting the horrors of death all around you before you realize that you were so wrong about what you could do. I don't even know why we thought we could make a difference. And in the end, I don't think we did."

Just listening to Thomas while he told his war stories was all I could do. I couldn't comment, I couldn't agree or disagree. Because I didn't know. I was in the presence of the man who had suffered so much more than I could ever imagine. But what Thomas needed was support, someone to listen to what he had to say. And I would do that for him.

"It was Claire's letters that pulled me through," Thomas said. "Knowing that there was someone out there, alive and waiting for me was what drove me on some days when everything else was failing. When I had lost everyone else."

How would I feel if I had to go to war and Amelia was waiting for me? I imagined I would hold onto her the same way Thomas had held onto my gran. It all just made the fact that they had lost each other just that much more tragic.

"I lost all my friends back then," Thomas said, as he eyes became watery. "I met all of them at the base, and we became close so quickly. And when you lose a life, when you see people die in front of your eyes—" Thomas couldn't finish his sentence, his voice caught in his throat. I reached out and squeezed his arm, wishing I could offer him more comfort. But this was something I knew about. Thomas was fighting his own demons and no one could help him with that.

I felt Amelia sliding her hand into mine and squeezing. She wasn't the part of this conversation, but even so, she was just as supportive and had my back as much as ever.

Chapter 12

Dane

WHEN THE PLANE TOOK off, I could see that Thomas was really battling. He grabbed the armrests so tightly that his knuckles turned white and he squeezed his eyes shut. I put my hand on his arm, trying to be there for him. And I could hear him let out the smallest breath, almost inaudibly, but I knew that he knew I was there.

I wished I could do more for him, and be there for him in different ways. But I also knew that struggling with trauma and battling the demons of the past was a very lonely journey. No one could help you through it. Not even therapists and psychologists, though I had been to both numerous times. I had been to therapy for months, yet still felt like I had been fighting the battle alone.

Until I met Amelia. She had changed everything for me. She had distracted me from the past by giving me a future to look forward to.

Hopefully, we were doing the same for Thomas and we could give some of his past back to him. Perhaps even some of the happiness he had lost. So that he would have a future, too. No one deserved to die alone and both Thomas and my gran had so much to catch up on, so much time to make up for.

Thomas didn't relax until the seatbelt sign kicked off. He was white around the mouth, his eyes wide, rolling in their sockets.

"It's going to be fine now, Thomas," I said again. But even as I said it, I knew that it wasn't going to help.

"I need a drink," Thomas said, hoarsely.

I nodded and lifted my hand to flag the air hostess.

"We are going to come past with an opportunity to buy drinks in a moment," she said kindly. And I had known that, of course, but was trying get it done sooner.

"Please, my friend here is really struggling. If you could maybe just make an exception for us."

The air hostess was going to argue with me, I could already see it. But then she glanced at Thomas and something about the way he looked made her nod, instead.

"I'll be right back," she said.

She came back with a plastic glass filled with two fingers of amber liquid. Whiskey. Thomas took the glass from her and threw it back before the air hostess could disappear again. He took a deep breath and held it in for a couple of counts before he let it out loudly.

"Thank you," he said to me.

I nodded. "I know what it's like, trust me."

Thomas frowned. "What? How do you know?"

I glanced at Amelia who had just put on her earphones and closed her eyes. I knew that she was checking out of this conversation on purpose, giving me and Thomas some private time. I appreciated that about her, she was so sensitive to what we needed. It was yet another thing about her that I absolutely adored.

"I am a police officer and several months ago, I was in the middle of a shooting."

Thomas raised his eyebrows. Even just saying those words made me feel anxious. I drummed my fingers on the armrest and Thomas glanced down.

"I see," he said, and I knew he understood. "If you want to share, feel free. But I know it's not always that easy."

"It's not," I said. "But sometimes, it helps to talk." I thought back to the night in the park where I had told Amelia everything that had happened to me. I hadn't meant to pour everything out to her, but she had been such a good listener, and afterward, I had felt so much lighter.

"It was just a normal day. The sun was shining, the weather was great and I was bantering with my partner at the station. Seems like these things always happen on good days, don't they?"

Thomas nodded.

"Anyway, we got a call that there was an armed robbery situation at the convenience store. There were hostages, the whole spiel. Police were already on scene but they needed backup."

I took a deep breath, going back in time to that day. I heard Drew's voice telling me that we should hurry up, the way he bantered back and forth, telling me that it was about time something happened in this little town.

Damn, if he had only known.

"By the time we arrived, the police that had been at the scene had been shot." I tried not to remember the slumped body on the tarmac, and how it had hit me in the gut as if I had personally been shot. It had become personal so quickly.

"The kid inside, damn, he was so young. And waving a gun around like he didn't know what the hell to do with the thing. But clearly he knew, because he had already shot a couple of people at that point. We couldn't afford to wait for backup, there were still people in the store and the kid was really crazy. I just knew he was going to take more of them out and I didn't want to lose more innocent lives."

Thomas nodded as I spoke and I had a feeling that he understood. There was something different about talking to someone who had been through something similar. Someone who understood the pain and the trauma, and the decisions he had to make on the fly. War was hardly the same as a shooting in a convenience store, but the result was the same in some ways. We had both walked away from it as different people, stunned by what had happened, and forever changed.

"I asked Drew to cover me so I could go in and take care of this little punk. Just before that, we were arguing about how important it was, wondering if we could afford to wait for backup or if he'd kill more hostages. I was the one that pushed to go in." I swallowed, a lump rising in my throat. I still felt responsible for Drew's death. If I had only waited for backup, if I hadn't decided to go in, Drew might still be alive today.

But I couldn't keep doing that. I couldn't keep blaming myself. And I couldn't keep turning back to something I couldn't change. Drew was gone. I had lost my best friend. And that was something I was going to have to deal with for the rest of my life.

"What happened?" Thomas asked, and I realized that I was retreating into myself, replaying the event in my mind without speaking.

"The kid started shooting when I reached him, a bullet hitting me in the chest, in the shoulder. I went down, hard, and he got away. At least, that was what I thought. When Drew came to check if I was all right, I told him to go out back. I told him to take the kid down before he killed anyone else. Drew didn't want to go, he wanted to stay with me to make sure I would be fine."

I had to stop talking and swallow once, twice, three times. My voice had become thick and caught in my throat every now and then. I felt like I was on the verge of a breakdown. But at the same time, I wasn't. I was reliving everything that had happened to me, but I was in charge here. I was in control of my emotions. It hadn't happened like this before, and for the first time, I felt like I was just telling the story and not reliving it moment by moment.

That fact caught me off guard. I had thought I would be imprisoned by my past forever.

"He went after him. Drew was such a great partner. So damn brave. But the kid hadn't gotten away, and didn't run as I thought. He was still there and he—he shot Drew. By the time I managed to drag myself to his side, he was already gone. I never even got to say goodbye."

In my mind, I could hear the voices of the EMT's shouting over the wail of sirens, and could see more blue uniforms flooding the convenience store. Lights were flashing in my eyes, and someone was putting pressure on the bullet wounds that hurt like a bitch. I remember tasting blood in my mouth, and reaching out, groping across the floor, trying to find Drew, to touch him.

But all they kept telling me was that he was gone.

"I'm so sorry to hear about your pain," Thomas said, and it pulled me back to the present. I looked around the plane and it felt strange to be sitting here, just like everyone else. Thomas and I had lived through events that few people around us experienced. We carried pain and trauma with us when everyone else was smiling.

But in a way, I felt connected to Thomas. Because we had been through the same kind of pain. Because we understood each other.

"It still affects me every day," I told Thomas. "And it probably will for a long time. Loud noises set my teeth on edge. I still try to avoid convenience stores if I can help it. When I have to go in, I always look around like a lunatic. Frantic, and scared that something might go wrong. Intellectually, I know that I'm fine, but that all goes out the window in those moment. Sometimes, I even catch myself scanning the crowds for concealed weapons."

Thomas was nodding as I talked and I knew he could relate. We hadn't experienced the same forms of trauma, and didn't have the same triggers, but clearly we were in the same boat.

"It never ends, does it?" I asked.

Thomas looked at me and finally, he smiled. And it was so good to see the smile on their face again. I was worried that he wouldn't smile at all, and that the entire plane trip would be traumatic for him.

"No, it doesn't end, son. But the older you get, the closer you become to none of it mattering anymore."

His words hit me hard. They were incredibly sad. To live an entire life and go through so much, only to have it mean nothing in the end just seemed wrong. But that was what life without love became, wasn't it? Thomas didn't have a family that he could turn to. People that could support him, and love him the way a family loved each other. Since he had lost my grandmother, Thomas had been alone. Sure, he had siblings, and they had children. He had people who cared for him.

But it wasn't the same. And I was so incredibly sad for him. Again, I hoped that this trip would change things. I hoped that my gran would be accepting of the visit, and that she would be inviting. I hoped that she would be the support and the love he needed, just as I hoped he would be the same for her.

It was still a bit of a question. I had no idea what would happen once we arrived in Pinewood and took Thomas to see my gran. But in my gut, I just knew that the moment she saw Thomas, she would forget everything and fly into his arms. Thomas had lit up exactly the same way when we had told him about her—that she was still alive and he could meet her.

This was the last leg of our journey, and I was so looking forward to it being a happy ending. Now more than ever.

Chapter 13

Claire
1955

HOW LONG HAD IT BEEN since I had been inside a bar? I tried to calculate, and with a shock I realized that the very last time might have been in London. I didn't believe I had been to a bar with Reggie since I had arrived in America. After all, I was the perfect little housewife, so a bar was no place for a lady like me.

Well, how had I ended up here, then? Perhaps I wasn't quite the person Reggie believed I was.

No, I knew for a fact that I wasn't. I hadn't been since the start of our marriage. I had been pregnant when we got married, with another man's child. And I had never told him that the child was not his. All this time, I had tried to be the perfect housewife that Reggie wanted, conforming to the American dream. But I had never really been that person at all.

It seemed almost right that I was here in a bar, the betrayal complete.

I sipped a martini, listening to the music that floated around me from invisible speakers. The air smelled like smoke and I thought of Thomas. I always associated that smell with him, even though Reggie sometimes smoked cigars. It just wasn't the same.

A man took the stool next to me. I glanced at him and he was incredibly handsome. Square jaw, blonde hair, deep-set eyes. He was upright, too. And he ordered a whiskey. Not a beer, like Reggie always drank. Why did I find that so attractive, all of a sudden?

I pressed my hand against my pocket where I could feel the weight of my wedding ring, an unpleasant reminder screaming at me. This was so very wrong. I shouldn't have been looking at another man. I shouldn't have compared him to Reggie and found Reggie lacking. I should have been back home, doing what I needed to do.

The problem was, I didn't care anymore. I wasn't sure how long it had been since I had. I was feeling comfortably numb at the moment, and it wasn't only the alcohol. I had felt like this for a while now, numb and uncaring, dead to the world. Maybe that was why it was so easy for me to be here. And why the feeling of the alcohol surging through my veins was so welcome. It made me feel a little more alive again.

"Well, good evening," the man said to me. "What is a beautiful woman like you doing in a place like this?"

I didn't roll my eyes at him. It was a very cliché line, but I liked having a bit of attention.

"Just looking for a breather," I said. "And perhaps a bit of attention."

The man grinned at me. "I happen to have a bit of extra attention lying around." He held his hand out to me. "I'm Robert. Robert Price. But you can call me Bob."

"Bob," I said with a smile. "Claire."

I didn't add my last name. I didn't know if Bob would associate me with Reggie if he knew my last name. I didn't want him to be able to look me up and find out who I was, or that I was married.

"Now that is a beautiful name if I ever heard one," Bob said. "Perfect to describe a beautiful woman."

His lines were so cliché, all of them, but despite myself, I blushed. I liked that someone thought I was beautiful again, and alluring. It made me feel warm, and alive for the first time in a very long while. It reminded me of the time at the bar when I had met Thomas, but this wasn't quite the same. No one would ever make me feel the way Thomas had.

I pushed the thought of him away. If I thought about Thomas now, I would get up and walk away from Bob. Because no one would ever be Thomas and it would be ridiculous for them to try.

"Do you mind?" Bob asked, before lighting a cigar. I shook my head. Well, a gentleman. What do you know?

"So, tell me," I said, trying to make conversation. "What do you do?"

"I am a stockbroker," he said. "I work in the city, coming back home after hours."

"That sounds like a lot of driving," I said.

Bob nodded. "It is, but I don't want to live in the city. Too stifling. I would rather live in Pinewood. It's beautiful here and I like the people."

I liked Bob. I liked the way he spoke, and his accent was thicker than Reggie's. He pronounced his words in a way that rolled off the tongue. His voice was deep and smooth. Silky.

As he spoke, I realized that he had money. A lot of money. He wasn't scared to rub it in my face, either. But I didn't mind. I wasn't here looking for a soulmate, a life partner. It didn't matter that Bob had flaws. I had many flaws myself. Too many, in fact.

We continued talking. Bob liked talking about himself. But I didn't mind. I liked listening. Besides, I didn't have that much to share about myself anyway. After all, what did I have to offer? I was a housewife, with no hobbies and no interests. Not anymore. So much of me had died out. And even if I'd had something to share, I didn't want to reveal too much of who I was.

I didn't want him to think I was a terrible person for what I was doing, either. How I would be able to explain that all I needed was a bit of love? All I needed was to feel important again. Noticed, and real. It had been so long since I had felt anything at all, and I just needed to feel alive again.

As the night continued, Bob and I drank together. He bought me drinks, keeping my glass full, and I didn't complain. I had one drink after the other, acting the way Reggie would, not caring about my limits. The alcohol burned in my veins, making my head feel light and airy. It made me care even less than I already did.

I stopped worrying about who might see me here. I stopped thinking about Junior and where he might be. I stopped thinking about Reggie, passed out on the couch at home, possibly waking up and noticing I was gone.

All I thought about was how Bob made me feel, and how I didn't want this feeling to end. Even if it was watered down compared to what I had before. Even if it wasn't what I really craved at all.

By the time Bob and I stepped out of the bar, the night felt like ice on my skin and it took my breath away. Bob put his arm around me and I leaned against him, searching for warmth. I took a deep breath and smelled his cologne. It was foreign in my nostrils, but I liked it. It was attractive, a turn on. When I looked up at Bob, he looked down at me and the distance between us suddenly seemed non-existent. His face was very close to mine.

And then Bob lowered his face and kissed me.

There were no fireworks. There was no heat that erupted inside me. There was no magic dancing on my skin. This was not love.

It was pure lust. Because I did want more of this. I wanted the attention. I wanted the adoration.

"It might seem very untoward of me to ask," Bob said. "But would you like to come home with me?"

"I would," I said, nodding.

With his arm around my waist, Bob escorted me to his car. It was a large car, very fancy. In the darkness I couldn't tell what it was, but Bob opened the passenger door for me and I slid into leather seats. Bob climbed in behind the steering wheel. It flashed in my mind that he had been drinking, but I didn't care. I was living life on the edge, and danger was my middle name. For the first time, I was taking chances.

If something went wrong? Well, so be it.

Nothing went wrong. Bob drove out of town, heading up against one of the hills on the other side. It was so far removed from my own life, I loved it.

When Bob finally pulled into his driveway, I gaped up at the house. I lived in the lap of luxury with Reggie, with quite a bit of money to spend. We had the latest cars and clothes, and Junior would never want for anything. But this? This was on a whole different level.

"Is everything alright?" Bob asked.

I turned to him and nodded. "Everything is perfect."

Maybe that was a lie. It wasn't quite perfect. But this would do. It was closer than my life was, considering that everything I had at home was on the verge of collapse.

Bob opened my door for me and offered me a hand, helping me out of the car. I stumbled, the alcohol affecting my balance, and Bob caught me. My body was pressed up against his and I giggled. He kissed me again. I tasted whiskey and the cigar on his breath. But his hand ran down my back and I shivered.

I wanted this, I realized. I wanted the release.

Bob led me into his house. It was almost like a museum, with double volume ceilings and all the walls covered in expensive paintings. Bob gave me a short tour of the house, showing off his riches. And I said all the right things at the right times, encouraging him, stroking his ego. But the honest truth was that I didn't care about his money and his house. When I cared about was his attention.

Eventually, Bob felt that I had seen enough and he pulled me against him again and kissed me.

"I don't believe I showed you my bedroom," he said, in a sultry voice.

"No, I don't believe you did," I said, with a smile.

Bob took my hand and led me through the giant house, through a maze of passages and rooms until we were finally in the master bedroom. The room was so much larger than I had ever seen, even larger than my living room. In the middle of the room stood a four-poster bed, with couches huddled around a window as if it was a private little sitting-room.

Bob closed the door and turned to me.

"I'm going to be honest with you," he said to me. "Since the moment I saw you, I wanted this. I hope that it doesn't offend you."

I shook my head. "It doesn't. Because I feel the same way. I have been attracted to you since the moment we met."

The conversation continued, and I was seeing myself as a third person in the room. This wasn't who I was, I thought.

Bob kissed me again and this time, he started undressing me. I allowed him, giving myself over to what we were doing. Because this was what I had wanted all along. This was what I had left the house for, what I had needed.

While Bob undressed me, I tried to give myself over to the feeling. Eventually, I managed to switch off the part of my mind that thought rationally and slipped into the person I was becoming. Because, maybe this was who I was, after all.

Chapter 14

Thomas

BY SOME MIRACLE, I survived the flight. I knew that I had been overreacting when I was getting on that plane, but I just couldn't help how unraveled I felt. After all, it had been the first plane I had gotten on in fifty years. It was nothing short of terrifying.

Not to mention that everything had changed so much since then. The world had moved on, so much faster than I had thought. Everything was fancier, upgraded, more efficient and confusing. Loaded with technology I didn't understand. I felt like I was in some kind of space age plane, riding a ship that would take me to the moon.

When we touched down on the runway, I felt like I was going to cry. But I kept it together. Not only because I felt like a fool for acting this way, but because Dane and Amelia were being so incredibly kind toward me. Especially Dane, who had stuck with me during the entire flight, making sure that I was okay. And thanks to him, I really was. More okay than I would have been otherwise.

I hadn't thought that looking back at the war and revisiting those memories would make me feel the way it had. Usually, when I thought back to those days, it left me feeling hollow, worn out, used and spat out. Gone were the days when I trembled with anxiety, when I felt like I couldn't escape the nightmares, and when it sounded like the gunfire was all around me once again. I hadn't had spells like that for a while, now. But still, talking about the war never made me feel all right.

Discussing it with Dane, however, had been different. It was different speaking to someone who understood. For the first time in my life, someone understood when I said that I was terrified about something that didn't make sense. Perhaps because I had gone home to ~~the~~ Montana and stayed there, I had never been surrounded by any other war veterans, not since the day I left England.

Dane wasn't a war veteran, of course, but he had been through his fair share of pain. And I felt for the poor boy. To struggle so much at such a young age, he reminded me so much of myself. In so many ways. And God bless him, I was so grateful for this man and his wonderful Amelia.

It took us awhile to collect our luggage at the baggage carousel and finally, we had it all in a pile on the curb and Dane dashed off to get his vehicle from the parking lot. Once we were all settled into his truck, we headed for Pinewood.

"Are there any good hotels in Pinewood, or should I stay in one a little further away and come through?" I asked.

"Oh, no," Amelia cried out. "You are not going to stay in a hotel. You can stay with us."

"Yes, my apartment is more than big enough and I have a guest room all set up. Please, don't isolate yourself by staying in a hotel room. I would be honored to have you as my guest."

"Are you sure I'm not imposing?"

Dane and Amelia both shook their heads.

"I prepared a room for you," Dane said again. "It will be wonderful to have your company."

I was still a little apprehensive, but Dane and Amelia were both so eager. And of course, if they had traveled to Montana to come to find me, it wasn't surprising that they had prepared for the scenario in which I had agreed to accompany them back to Pinewood.

"Okay," I finally agreed. I was still a little unsure—everything here was so new and unfamiliar. But perhaps it would be better to stay with

Dane, someone I knew, than being holed up in a hotel room somewhere. The promise of familiarity drew me and Dane and Amelia had both been so incredibly kind.

"I think we need to pick up a take out dinner on the way home," Amelia said. "I don't know about you two, but I don't feel like cooking tonight."

"That's an excellent idea," Dane agreed. And I had to admit, I liked the idea, too.

"What do you like?" Dane asked me.

"Oh, don't go out of your way for me, I'm just an old man. You two choose and I'll have whatever you do."

Amelia shook her head. "Surely you like something, too? Just because you're older than us doesn't mean you don't have your own taste! What will it be?"

"Well, I do really like Italian," I admitted.

Dane slapped his thigh. "Italian it is."

On the way, we stopped at Italian restaurant and Dane ran inside. He disappeared for a while and Amelia and I sat in the truck together.

"I just want to thank you again for doing all of this for me," I said to her. "This journey has been a little daunting so far, I don't think I would have been able to get through it without the two of you helping me."

Amelia reached for me and squeezed my hand. She had such a lovely smile.

"It's our pleasure," she said. "I sincerely hope that this trip will pay off for you. It's so important to be happy."

I nodded. "That, my dear, will get you far in life. If happiness is the goal of everything you do, you can never go wrong."

Amelia and I smiled at each other. We sat in silence in the cab for the rest of the time Dane was inside, but it was a comfortable silence, amicable. I didn't feel out of place and uncomfortable, I didn't feel nervous and unsure. I didn't know what it was about these kids, but they made me feel like I was home, even though I wasn't.

Come to think of it, I hadn't really felt at home in a very long time. Not even when I had actually been at home on the ranch.

Dane finally appeared again with three paper bags. He climbed inside the truck and the smell of basil and tomato paste filled the cab. Amelia groaned, commenting on how good it smelled.

The truck pulled out again and we completed the last bit of our journey.

When we arrived, I helped carry the food up while Dane and Amelia brought their luggage and mine. Dane's apartment was neat and tidy, though a bit sparse, with little furniture and paintings. It seemed almost clinical, and somehow, it was a space I could completely relate to.

After Dane showed me to my room, which was a quaint little guestroom he had made up especially for me. There was a bed by the window and a desk where I could sit and write if I chose to. Then we all came together in the kitchen. Amelia had dished up the food we had ordered and we sat around the kitchen island.

Dane had ordered me a fettuccine Alfredo, and honestly it was one of the best meals I'd had in a long time. Dane and Amelia drank a bit of wine with their meal, but I had chosen lemonade instead. I didn't drink much alcohol these days, and I didn't want to be out of sorts. Tomorrow was a very big day for me.

"I can't believe we're here," Amelia said. "Here's to us." She lifted her wine glass. Dane and I lifted our glasses as well and we clinked them together.

"To a wonderful journey, no matter how this ends up," Dane said.

I had to agree.

"Do you mind if we ask you about Claire?" Amelia asked.

"My dear child, you've earned the right to ask me anything."

Amelia and Dane glanced at each other.

"We were just wondering what it was like for you when you met her. Dane told me that from his grandmother's side, everything had been stars and roses. Pure happiness. To her, it was love at first sight and just magic. Was it the same for you?"

I sat back a little on the stool and thought back to the time I had met Claire in the bar.

"I didn't go out to meet girls that night," I said. "In fact, I didn't really want to go out at all, but my friends dragged me along, saying that it was the last time we would be able to enjoy ourselves for a while. Looking back, they were right of course. And boy, was I ever glad that I went. When I walked into that bar and locked eyes with her, I knew it was all over for me."

Closing my eyes, I could still smell the smoke in the bar, and hear the music floating in the background. I could still feel the warmth on my skin when Claire had come over to me, buying me a drink as if she was in charge. Instantly, I had known that she was the woman I wanted for the rest of my life. The rest of the night, with Claire showing me around town and the easy conversations we had, it was all a formality.

"I hadn't believed in love at first sight before that," I said. "But with her, everything was different. She challenged everything I believed in, and made everything in life seem different. And when you experience something like that, there is no going back."

Dane and Amelia glanced at each other again, Amelia's eyes full of stars. I knew that whatever was between these two, they could relate so strongly to my story. And it made me happy. It made me so happy to know that these two had found love in a way that very few people got to experience.

"What was it like, having to go to war after meeting her like that?" Dane asked.

"Having to leave her behind was pure torture," I admitted. "I felt incomplete, like I'd left a part of me behind in London. We promised to wait for each other, so that after the war, I could take her back home to my ranch and we would live happily ever after. That's the fairytale isn't it? That's the dream."

But it hadn't happened that way. We hadn't made it. I hadn't been able to find Claire after the war. The heaviness sank down over the conversation and I knew Dane and Amelia were thinking the same thing.

"Her letters got me through the hardest times when I was at war," I said. "Even though, after a while, I stopped receiving them. I still reread the first letters she had sent me, holding onto her words, able to recite them in my sleep. She was what I was living for, what I was staying alive for when things got really tough. So many of my friends died around me, but I had to get back to Claire. I couldn't afford to die on the battlefield. I couldn't leave her waiting. It was all her, getting me through. She was the reason I survived."

A sadness lay heavy on my chest and I took a deep breath, trying to get rid of it again. I tried not to think of the life I could have had with Claire, tried not to think of all the years I'd spent without her, pining away and thinking that she hadn't wanted me anymore.

As if the kids understood how I felt, they changed the topic and steered the conversation in a happier direction. We ate our meal, drank, laughed and talked. And by bedtime, I felt like a younger man again.

When I went to bed, I was brimming with excitement. Nerves, too, because tomorrow was going to be a big day and the results were uncertain. I didn't know what to expect from Claire, or how it would be meeting her again after so many years. But I was more excited than nervous. I had waited decades for this day and thought it would never come. But now that it was finally here, I was ready to embrace it. I wasn't going to let her slip through my fingers a second time, not unless it was what she wanted.

I lay in bed, thinking about everything that had led me here, and how it had happened that I was in Pinewood, Oklahoma. Dane and Amelia were wonderful people.

When I closed my eyes, I saw Claire in front of me again, with her dark hair and dark eyes and those ruby red lips. And she was smiling at me the way she used to. Happy to see me. In love.

Chapter 15

Amelia

DANE AND I LAY IN HIS bed, facing each other. We had come to bed hours ago, but we were still awake, quietly talking. This was something I loved about him so much. I could spend time with Dane in any way, whether it be on a date, talking about difficult things in the past, sleeping together, or just talking. Everything with him was amazing.

It was also great to be in his apartment. I had never stayed over at his place before, we'd always gone to mine. So this felt like a step in our relationship—if that was what it was. We weren't exactly official, but I saw Dane as my guy, and the way he treated me was as if I was his girl.

And I liked it.

"I can't believe we've come this far," I said, though I must have said it a million times, already. "And to think that Thomas agreed to come with us, I just can't seem to wrap my mind around it. When we took that letter to your grandmother and she was so hostile about it, I thought for sure that was it. But look where we are now!"

"I know," Dane said. "The whole thing seems so surreal. Now we just need to do the final step, we need to get Thomas and my gran together."

"I'll admit, I have no idea what to expect," I said.

"Yeah, me either. But I have a great feeling about this. It couldn't all have worked out so beautifully just to blow up in our faces now. Everything happens for a reason and I think that this is going to be a good thing."

I nodded, and we lay there in silence for a while. I wondered how Claire would react when she saw Thomas. I wondered how Thomas would react toward her. Everything we were doing was like it was straight out of a love story. Like a movie or a book. It was difficult to believe that all of this was real and that it was truly happening right in front of our eyes.

"What if she doesn't want to see him?" I asked. After all, she had wanted nothing to do with the letter. But this was different now, wasn't it?

"I'm sure she'll want to see him. This isn't like a letter we are dropping in her lap. This is Thomas, the man she was head over heels in love with. As soon as he stands in front of her, nothing else will matter. This is years and years of waiting, and all the pining away and wondering will finally come to an end. And the loveless lives they both have lived will be over."

I thought about the plane trip here, and the conversations between Dane and Thomas.

"Can I ask you something?" I asked.

"Of course," Dane said. "You know you can ask me anything."

"I heard you and Thomas talking about the war and the shooting on the plane," I said. "I tried to stay out of it, giving you two some alone time. But I just—well, are you okay?"

Dane was silent for the longest time. For a moment, I thought he might have fallen asleep, or worse that I'd offended him. But then, he spoke.

"It was difficult to talk about, I have to admit. But I felt like it was important. Thomas was struggling so much with everything he had been through, the trip on the plane particularly. It's difficult to explain."

"I heard what he said," I continued. "And I get it, to the extent that I'm able, anyway. But what about you? How are you feeling?"

I sensed that Dane was trying to avoid answering me. And that made me even more worried.

"Honestly, I'm terrified," Dane said. "I am so scared that things will never go back to how they used to be before the shooting. I'm scared that this anxious, nervous, paranoid person is who I am now. And that the memories and nightmares and everything else that comes with this PTSD will never go away. I mean, I look at Thomas and I see a shell of the man he used to be. Of course, I didn't know him. And who knows what he had all gone through. But I'm scared that this is my new normal, and that this is the reality I'll have from now on."

I thought about it for a moment. "Is that the worst-case scenario?" I asked.

"What do you mean?" Dane asked. "That things might not go back to how they were?"

"Yeah," I said into the dark.

"I guess so," Dane said. "I mean, I can't imagine anything worse than this."

"I understand," I said, and curled closer to Dane, throwing my arms over his chest, letting him know that he wasn't alone. "But that's true of a lot of things, isn't it? I mean, things will never be the same for Thomas and Claire. Even if they have a happy ending now, they won't be the people they were when they met each other. And Thomas, things will never be the same for him after the war, either. Or for Claire, after her marriage. And I'm afraid that things might never be the same for you, either. But these are the things that make us. The good and the bad. They shape who we are, and help us to grow. And that is not such a bad thing, is it? After all, the person you are now, is the person that I love spending time with so much."

Dane rolled onto his side toward me and it pressed our bodies against each other. "You are such a breath of fresh air, Amelia. You have a way of explaining things so simply, making it easy to understand, easy to accept. You have no idea how much you mean to me."

"I'm so glad I can help," I said. "As long as you understand that I am here for you, no matter what."

Dane pulled me against him, his arms around me, and he kissed me. Heat grew between us, flooding both our bodies, and the kiss became urgent almost right away.

I ran my hand down Dane's back and he cupped my breast. I sighed into his mouth. I loved the way he touched me, like I was special, and to be revered somehow. And like he would never get used to me.

Dane slid his tongue into my mouth, tasting me, exploring me while his hands roamed my body.

I pushed my hands under his shirt and worked it up. He let go of me long enough for me to pull it over his head, before his hands were on me again. We lay in bed, pressed tightly together, our hands running over each other's bodies. I couldn't get enough of him.

After a while of kissing and groping, I gently pushed Dane over on his back and pulled myself up onto him. My body was pressed along the length of his and I felt every inch of him, as well as his erection, evidence of his want and need for me. I ground my hips against him, my breasts against his chest so he could feel me.

Dane ran his hands up my sides.

"You're amazing," he whispered. "Beautiful in every way, inside and out."

I kissed him again. My hand slid down his neck and onto his shoulder and I touched the messy ridge of scar tissue.

"Do you hate it?" he asked, speaking into the dark. My heart clenched.

"Of course not," I said. "I don't hate anything about you. This defines you the way everything else about you does. And I care very much for you. Every part of you."

Dane let out a shaky breath, as if he had expected a different answer.

It was so sad that he still thought he wasn't worth loving. But I didn't see it that way. Everything about Dane was a part of who he was and I adored him—even the parts that were imperfect. Especially the parts that were imperfect.

I shifted on top of him and placed my lips on his scar, kissing him. I moved slowly over his chest onto the other scar, before making my way down his body. I kissed his stomach, and the sculpted muscles that led down his torso. I tugged his boxers down when I reached the waist band and his cock stood erect and eager.

But I didn't give it my attention, not yet. Instead, I worked his boxers down his legs, just enough to give me room to work with, and I kissed him all around his sex. His thighs, his hips, his stomach. Until he was squirming underneath me, dying with anticipation.

"You're driving me crazy," Dane gasped.

I licked the head of his dick and Dane sucked his breath in through his teeth. When I took the head of his cock into my mouth, he moaned and I moved up and down, sliding him in and out of my mouth, moving my tongue. I swirled it around his head a few times before sinking down again.

Dane groaned and pushed his hands into my hair. He guided me down onto his cock and back up again, allowing me the freedom to do what I was doing, while telling me how much he wanted it, and how much he was enjoying it, just by the way he curled his hands into fists, bunching my hair in his hands.

After a while of sucking him, worshiping him with my mouth, I slipped his dick out of my mouth and kissed him again, moving up his body. Before I straddled him, I got rid of my pants. I sat on top of him without him pushing into me just yet, and I pulled my tank top over my head. Dane looked up at me, his eyes dark with lust, his lips parted and his eyes trailing slowly over my body.

His hands were on my hips. I leaned forward and kissed him.

And while I did, I reached between us, took hold of his dick, and guided him to my entrance.

When I sat down on him, we both moaned. I braced my hands on the pillow on either side of his head and pushed myself even further down, burying him inside of me.

When I started moving my hips, I moaned, trying to keep it down. Thomas was in the house, probably fast asleep.

Dane's hands were still on my hips and when I started rocking back and forth, he helped me, pulling me forward further than I could go, rocking me back harder. His brows knit together as if he was concentrating and his lips were parted, his face stunningly handsome in the dim lighting in the room.

I rocked harder and faster, riding him. Tonight was all about Dane, about what I felt for him and how it translated between us. And I wanted to show him that no matter what he'd been through and no matter what he looked like, he was still perfect to me.

I finished fast. My clit had been rubbing against his pubic bone and with his dick so deep inside me, I hadn't been able to hold off.

And tonight, Dane was right there with me. He was incredibly close in no time at all. I could tell by the way he breathed that he was on the verge.

"How do you do this to me?" he asked. But it was a rhetorical question, one I couldn't answer because the moment he said it, he released inside of me, stomach muscles clenching so that he curled up. I felt him pumping into me and it triggered an echo of the orgasm I just had. I cried out, not trying to be quiet anymore. Dane moaned too as we orgasmed together. Again.

I loved that we always did this.

I slowed down when I knew that Dane was coming down from his orgasm and he would be sensitive. My body trembled all over, my breathing coming in ragged gasps. I lowered myself onto his chest, then kissed him before turning my head and laying it on his shoulder and heard his heartbeat hammering against my ear for a while.

When Dane eventually was soft inside of me, I lifted myself up and let him slip out before I lay down next to him on the bed.

He kissed me on the forehead, but we didn't say anything to each other. Sometimes, there were no words to be had.

Chapter 16

Claire

WHEN I WOKE UP, IT was at the crack of dawn. The sun still wasn't up, but the sky was gray with the promise of a new day.

I was in bed next to Bob, the large poster bed rising around me and there was distance between me and Bob. We might have slept together, but we weren't cuddling. We were not in love.

That was alright, though. Because I hadn't been in love with Reggie for years and we had done something similar, at least in the beginning.

I sat up, naked. Bob was still asleep. I stretched, relishing the feeling between my legs, the sexy sultry feeling in my body. This was what I had been after. I had wanted to be touched, to be felt, to be noticed. And Bob had given me exactly that.

Quietly, I found my clothes from last night. They were peppered across the floor, crumpled in piles I had left them. I pulled on my underwear, my skirt and then my blouse and finally, my coat. When I stepped into my shoes, Bob stirred under the sheets. I looked at him, but he let out a soft snore and continued sleeping.

For a moment, I wondered if I should wake him up to say goodbye. It seemed almost wrong to creep out of the house like this, like a criminal. I decided against waking him, but I fished around in my handbag and found a receipt for something. I scribbled my number on the back, writing times that I would be available. If he wanted to see me, it had to be at a time that Reggie wasn't home. I hoped that he would understand. I hadn't told him that I was married, but if we were going to do this again, he was going to find out at some point.

When I patted my pocket, I felt my wedding ring exactly where I had left it. Slipping it onto my finger, I left the room.

I made my way through the maze of corridors, finally finding the front door. I let myself out, relieved that the door wasn't locked, and walked down the drive. It wasn't a long walk before I came across a cab and flagged it down.

When I climbed in, I gave the driver my home address and he drove to the other side of town.

It was still extremely early when I opened my own front door and crept to the living room. Reggie was still passed out on the couch just where I had left him last night. I wondered if he had been in this position the whole night.

Putting my bag down, I walked to the bedroom. I climbed into the shower, washing my hair, scrubbing my body to get rid of any sign that I had been unfaithful. While I stood in the shower, I knew that I should feel guilty for what I had done. I was a terrible wife, after all.

But the fact was, I couldn't find it in myself to feel guilty. For the first time in a long time, I felt alive again.

When I climbed out of the shower, I walked to the bedroom with a towel around my body and around my hair as I chose clothes for the day. A neat little dress that buttoned down all the way in the front, low heels that went with it, and stockings. I dried my hair and styled it the right way, then spritzed on some perfume and put on my make-up.

By the time that Reggie woke up, he wouldn't know that I had been out of the house at all.

I was in the kitchen, busy making breakfast, when Reggie stumbled through the door.

"Morning, darling," I said brightly.

Reggie grumbled something and clutched at his head, probably uncomfortable after drinking so much last night.

"Your breakfast will be ready, soon. Can I get you something?"

"Something for my head, it's killing me," Reggie said.

Nodding, I opened the medicine cabinet, taking out tablets for him and pouring him a glass of tomato juice. I handed it to him and Reggie grunted, leaving the kitchen so I could continue with my work. Before, I would have begrudged the fact that I would have to take care of the household duties alone. But I didn't feel like that, now. I was happy doing what I needed to do. For the first time in a long time, I didn't feel neglected and forgotten.

Maybe by Reggie, but I had found a replacement.

Of course, this would never replace the love I craved or what I'd had with Thomas. But that was okay because it wasn't what I was looking for. All I wanted was to feel like a woman again.

Junior came home a little later, dropped off after staying over at his friend's house

"How was your visit, darling?" I asked Junior when he came into the kitchen to hug me.

"Fine thanks, Mom," he said, and disappeared again. I tried not to notice that he was short with me, that he didn't want to sit on the counter and tell me about his visit anymore. He was getting older, I told myself. It was normal that he didn't want to share his life with me anymore. At least, that was what I told myself. Because if I started worrying about my relationship with Junior on top of everything else, I wasn't going to be able to do this. There was nothing I could do to replace what I had with Junior the way that I'd just replaced what I should have had with Reggie.

When I had finished making breakfast, Junior and I sat at the table and ate together. Reggie took his food and walked to his office, ready to eat his breakfast alone. Again, it would have bothered me a lot before, but it didn't bother me in the slightest now.

"Tell me about your visit," I said to Junior. "Did you have fun? What did you get up to?"

Junior pulled up his shoulders. "We kicked a ball around, played with cars, we talked."

"What did you talk about?" I asked.

"You know, stuff that boys talk about," Junior said.

It was difficult to get any conversation out of him. It was difficult to talk to him at all. Again, I tried not to worry about it too much. After all, I was in a good mood today. For the first time in a long time, I felt good and I wanted to relish it for as long as I could. Because as much as I wanted more of this, as much as I would have liked to see Bob again, I still wasn't sure that I would.

I hadn't been faithful. I was doing something wrong. But I couldn't help how right it felt, how good it felt to do something for me.

After breakfast, I walked to the kitchen and washed the dishes. I went to collect Reggie's dishes from his office. He didn't even make eye contact with me. But Reggie wasn't angry with me. He had no reason to be, he had no idea what I had done. It was just how he always was with me. As if I was in the house to cook and clean and nothing else.

While I cleaned in the kitchen, I hummed a tune I hadn't even thought about in years. Come to think of it, I hadn't hummed or sang in a very long time.

It felt good to feel alive again. It felt good to have a small part of me back. Because that was what this was about. Regaining some of myself, finding part of myself that I thought I had lost.

It was good to know that I wasn't completely dead yet.

The rest of the day was spent cleaning and tidying up the house. On the weekend, Reggie was home, but I barely noticed him. He spent the day locked up in his office or outside tending to the roses and it was almost as if he was away at the office, anyway. Junior kept himself busy with his toys in his room, and I was left to do my own thing.

When I prepared lunch, Reggie came into the kitchen.

"What's for lunch?" He asked.

"I'm making club sandwiches," I said.

"And you're using that?" he asked, nodding to the ham.

"I thought it would be nice," I said.

"I would prefer turkey," Reggie said.

I looked at the sandwiches I had already prepared. I could give those to Junior or I would eat them myself.

"Okay, darling," I said, and I walked to the fridge, taking out turkey I had prepared.

"If that's what you would like, that's what you get."

I didn't say it with the same bitter tone I usually did. In fact, I didn't mind all that much that Reggie wanted something other than what I had already started preparing. After all, this was what he was like. He changed his mind all the time, and sometimes it felt like he was doing it on purpose, to grate on me. But nothing could get to me today. I wore a suit of armor, invisible to the naked eye.

For a while, Reggie watched me move around the kitchen, preparing our meals. Of course, he didn't offer to help. He never did. But again, I didn't mind. I would continue doing what I needed to do, ignoring him as much as I could.

"What's gotten into you?" He asked, frowning.

"What do you mean?" I replied innocently.

"You're different."

When I turned away from him, I had a smile. "Oh?" I asked.

Reggie was silent for a moment. "I don't know what it is but you seem a lot more upbeat."

"I'm sure I don't know what you're talking about," I said. "Lunch will be ready soon if you want to wash up."

Reggie mumbled something and left the kitchen. I was glad that he was leaving me be. I continued to finish our lunch, cutting the sandwiches just so, the way that Reggie liked them. Now that I had been unfaithful, I was going to do everything in my power to be perfect for Reggie, to do everything the way he wanted so there was absolutely nothing he could point out and scold me for. I was going to be the perfect housewife so he had nothing to criticize.

And then, when the time was right, I would escape again.

What had gotten into me, Reggie had asked. Well, how was I going to explain that? Of course, it had been Bob, the handsome stockbroker I had met last night. The man that made me feel alive again, touching me like a woman needed to be touched. But I wasn't going to say any of that to Reggie. I was just going to continue doing what I needed to do, and I was going to do it with a smile. Because that was what the perfect housewife did.

As long as I did exactly what I needed to, Reggie would be none the wiser. And if this was what it took for me to finally be happy, then so be it. So, what if I was doing something wrong? What if I was breaking all the rules? Who even said that they were rules anyway? What I needed to do now, was survive. And right now, this was what I needed to do to be able to retain my sanity.

Chapter 17

Thomas
1945

WHEN I WALKED INTO The Bell, everything looked different. And it wasn't just because I was someone else, now. The war had changed everything. I had heard from some people that The Bell had been closed for a long time. I was damn lucky it was open again.

Because this was where I wanted to have a drink. Where I had met Claire, the woman of my dreams.

I had only been in London for a day, but I wasn't going to waste any time before looking for her. And this was the first place, someone here had to know who she was. After all, she had been here a couple of times, even before she had met me.

"Have you seen Claire Whiteside?" I asked the barman.

"Who?" he replied.

"She used to come here frequently, dark hair, beautiful girl. About this high." I used my hand to show him.

The barman shook his head. "Everything is different since the war, buddy. You of all people should understand."

I was still wearing my soldier's uniform. He knew that I had been in battle, and that I had fought.

But even if I hadn't worn my uniform, he would be able to see it. I wasn't the man I used to be. I was broken, battered. I limped a little. I had scars on my face, my neck, and my arms. And when I looked at myself in the mirror, I seemed haunted. The war had broken me. I had been injured so many times, and every time I had hoped that it would be enough to send me home.

But that wasn't all. I had lost so many friends. Brothers. They had died all around me and I had watched every single one of them go. My soul was scarred, too.

"Please, does anyone know her?" I asked the few patrons who were drinking all around me.

Some of them didn't respond. Some of them looked up at me and only shook their heads.

"Hey, buddy, why don't you order yourself a drink and calm down?" the barman said.

I took a deep breath and let it out again, nodding. I might as well have a drink. I was anxious, paranoid. I was on edge, every nerve ending alive. When I heard the smallest sound, I jumped.

So I ordered a beer. Whenever someone walked through the doors, I asked them if they knew Claire Whiteside. But no one seemed to know who she was.

How was this possible? How could it be that no one had seen her? I knew that it had been three years, but she had told me that she would wait. She had promised.

It was that damn promise that had pulled me through everything. It was the only reason I was still alive. Because if I hadn't had Claire to return to, I would have given up ages ago. I would have died as well, next to all my friends, with no reason to keep living.

Despite asking again and again, and spending most of the day in the bar, no one knew Claire Whiteside, no one even knew the name. It should have been a powerful one, since she had told me that her father was a man of substance in the area.

But still, no one knew who I was talking about and I was starting to become agitated.

"Excuse me," someone said behind me and I spun around. In front of me stood a timid looking woman, with mouse brown hair that she had pulled back into a bun. She looked weary, with wide eyes and clothes that seemed a little tattered.

"Are you asking about Claire?"

"Yes!" I cried out, relieved that someone finally knew what I was saying. "Where is she? Is she alright? Is she alive?"

The woman looked around the bar as if she was worried about something.

"Come, sit with me," she said. "My name is Ruth."

"Thomas," I said.

"Yes, I remember," Ruth said.

But I didn't remember her. Still, I followed her to one of the booths in the back and we both sat down.

"I was Claire's friend for the longest time," Ruth said. "Even after Dorothy and Margaret left town, Claire and I still stuck together. It felt like everyone had abandoned us, then. But I understand it, now."

I nodded, impatient to hear what she had to say about Claire. But Ruth looked like she had been through her fair share of hell, and I didn't want to press her.

"Claire held on for the longest time, you have to understand that," Ruth said.

The way she said it made me worried. What did she mean she held on for the longest time? Had she been ill? Had she died? Fear clutched at my throat. What if I had done all of this for nothing? What if I had fought my way back only to realize that I had lost her, anyway? I didn't think I would be able to survive it. If it turned out that Claire was dead, I might as well kill myself, too. Because then my only reason for living would be gone.

"I don't know if you noticed, but everything has changed around here," Ruth continued. I wished she would just get to the point. But I knew well enough what war did, I had seen how people's minds had deteriorated. And I wasn't going to expect something from this woman that she wasn't able to offer. I wasn't going to expect a sound mind.

"I've noticed," I said. In fact, London had been shredded. So many buildings had been ruined, and the people looked like they had been to hell and back. Those that were alive seemed a little dazed to be so. And I could only imagine how many of them had died.

Please, let Claire not be one of them.

"Her father was worried for her safety. He tried to get them out of the city numerous times. Mister Whiteside," her voice caught in her throat and I expected the worst.

"They're dead, aren't they?" I blurted out.

Ruth nodded and my heart plummeted.

"Claire's parents, yes," Ruth said.

"And Claire?" I asked.

Ruth looked at me with eyes that were full of apologies.

"She held on for the longest time," Ruth said again.

"Why do you keep saying that?" I asked. "For Pete's sake, just tell me what happened. Put me out of my misery."

Ruth took a deep breath. "She was worried that you wouldn't come back. She was scared that you were already dead. And she didn't know what else to do."

"Do with what?"

"She met a businessman from America," Ruth said.

My whole body went cold. This was even worse than Claire dying. I felt like I couldn't breathe.

"Please, don't tell me—" I couldn't finish my sentence. I couldn't think straight.

"I'm so sorry, Thomas," Ruth said. "She left with him to go to America. A while ago, now. I think she married him."

My ears started ringing. My palms were sweaty and I felt lightheaded. This wasn't possible. How could this be?

"But she promised," I said to Ruth.

Ruth reached over the table and put her hand on mine. I yanked my hand away. I didn't want her sympathy, I didn't want her to tell me that she was sorry, that everything might be okay. I didn't want to hear another word from her. Who the hell did she think she was, bringing me news like this and thinking that everything was going to be fine between us?

"Are you going to be okay?" Ruth asked me.

"No!" I cried out. "I'm not going to be okay. How the hell am I supposed to be okay after hearing something like that? You know what it was like out there!?" I pointed, hoping that it was in the direction of Europe. "Do you know what kind of hell I've been through just to get back here?"

The more I shouted, the more Ruth shrunk in on herself, becoming small in her seat.

"Is there a problem here?" Another man asked, approaching us. I looked around and realized that everyone was staring at me. I was making a scene. And I was taking out my frustration and my pain and on Ruth, who hadn't done anything at all.

"No," I said to the man who stood next to me. "There is no problem here." I turned to Ruth. "I'm sorry. I shouldn't have exploded like that. It's just—" And then, I couldn't speak any more. Because if I wasn't screaming and shouting with rage, I was falling apart with sorrow. Because I had lost her. Claire had chosen someone else. She hadn't waited for me, she hadn't wanted me.

"She loved you, Thomas," Ruth said in a small voice.

"That's just the thing, isn't it?" I asked bitterly. "Loved. Past tense."

I dropped my head into my hands. I didn't know how long I sat there like that, but when I looked up again, Ruth was gone.

I didn't blame her. I was a mess. Physically, emotionally. Mentally.

The glass of beer I had ordered when Ruth had come to me was still half full and I grabbed it, downing the alcohol. I didn't usually drink like that, didn't throw alcohol down my throat as a remedy for what I was going through, but right now, I didn't think I was going to be able to cope any other way. As soon as the beer was finished, I walked to the bar and ordered another.

And then another, and another.

The time began to blur. People arrived as people left and I was the only one at the bar at times. I wondered when the barman was going to kick me out, and tell me I've had enough. Or tell me it was closing time. He did neither. Instead, he offered me the beers that I ordered, not saying anything at all.

Maybe he understood. Maybe he knew that losing something like this, losing someone like Claire to a man from America of all things—it hadn't even been a man from here, for Pete's sake—had shattered me. Maybe the barman understood that after coming back from the war, I had so little to cling to as it was.

Maybe he was just eager to take my money.

Whatever it was, I didn't care anymore. I drank until I stopped feeling. I drank until I stopped thinking.

And eventually, I drank until everything around me turned into a blur.

I wasn't sure what time it was when I finally decided that it might be a good idea to get back to the hotel room I had booked for myself when I had arrived in town. If I could even remember how to find the bloody hotel.

As I stumbled out of the bar, I heard the barman mutter something behind me. Maybe it was a question, but I didn't understand him.

All I wanted was to get out of here. Claire was gone and there was nothing left here for me. I had to get off this forsaken land and back to my home. There was nothing here for me. But back home, I could still make some kind of a living.

Although, that should have been with Claire, too. She had been a part of every single corner of my life. How had it happened so quickly? How had I fallen in love with her so completely?

But that didn't matter. What I had to do now was to try to get over her. I had to get her out of my mind, I had to get rid of the memories.

I had to find some other way to carry on.

Chapter 18

Amelia

WHEN I OPENED MY EYES, I was in Dane's bed. I hid a little deeper under the covers, snuggling in the warmth. Dane had an arm draped over my hip and it felt so right to be here. Everything about this was right, from the way I had met Dane, to the love letter, to the love story, and to where we were right now. So close to finding a happy ending. Not just for Claire and Thomas, but for me and Dane, as well.

My heart swelled with the feeling of contentment.

When I had left New York, I had been searching for a new life. I had felt stifled in the big city, unable to be the person I was meant to be.

I had chosen Pinewood because it was so quaint, so small, and perfect for what I needed. And I had known that the next big thing for me was waiting here.

But I sure hadn't thought that this was what would be waiting for me. I thought that it was my love for history that would be acknowledged, and I would find what my heart yearned for in that. The job at the antique store, after all, was exactly what I had been looking for.

But apparently that hadn't been what the universe had in store for me. At least, not only that.

Love had been just around the corner, too.

The letter I had found at the bottom of the box, the love story ruined by war. And Dane. It was all here, waiting for me all along. And I had only to come and find it.

I was so glad that I had. If it hadn't been for that letter, Dane and I would never have found each other. And if it hadn't been for the love story of Thomas and Claire, we would never had gotten so close. And now, with Thomas here in Pinewood, they were going to find their happy ending, too. I knew it.

And I couldn't wait.

So many people had told me that I was a fool for leaving New York City behind, for giving up my fast paced job and moving to Pinewood to settle down into something much slower. And a couple of times, I had doubted myself, too. I had wondered if I was doing the right thing by giving everything up I had worked for. I had given up the great apartment, said goodbye to a lot of friends. And my job had been a good one, even though I hadn't enjoyed it.

But coming to Pinewood had been the best decision ever. Not just because of everything I had found here, but because of everything I'd left behind. The person I had been in New York was not the person I wanted to be. And I had left that person behind.

It was perfect. I was so happy here. And I had a feeling that as time continued, I would only become even more so.

I slipped out of bed, careful not to wake Dane. I opened the bag I had packed to take to Montana, pulling on some clothes. But it was colder than I had expected, and I didn't have anything warmer. I shivered, thinking for a moment, before I tiptoed across the room and opened Dane's closet. I looked around, trying to find something that would work. Quickly, I settled on a sweatshirt. It was worn, something he must have had on a million times. The material was soft and even though it was clean, it still smelled like him. I pressed the material against my nose and breathed in.

This was the smell of happiness, I thought.

I pulled the sweatshirt over my head, pulled my hair into a ponytail, and left the apartment.

When I stepped into the cool morning air, I breathed deeply. Winter was on its way, I could smell the snow on the air. It wasn't here, yet. It wouldn't be for a while. But it was on the way. The turn of the season was always something I loved. The way that the earth anticipated the cold, the way that the trees slowly turned from green to oranges and yellows. And the way the winter danced on the wind, warning us of what was to come.

I didn't drive to the coffee shop. Instead, I walked. I liked being outside and as I went along, I greeted the few people that were already out on the street. I still had the day off, even though it was Tuesday, but everyone else was hurrying to get to work.

When I got to the coffee shop, there were a few people in line. I waited patiently to get to the front where Beth was serving today.

"Good morning!" Beth exclaimed when she saw me. "I didn't know you guys were back yet."

I nodded. "We got back last night.

"What will it be?" Beth asked.

I put in an order, a Chai Latte for me, a Hazelnut Latte for Dane, and a tall coffee with extra cream for Thomas.

"Recaps?" Beth asked after she logged order.

I nodded, fishing in my wallet for cash. "He's here, Beth. He came to Pinewood with us."

Beth blinked at me. "Thomas?"

I nodded, a giggle escaping my lips. I couldn't contain myself.

"Oh, my goodness," Beth said. "I can't believe that you guys managed it. You have to tell me everything."

"It's far too much to tell you while I'm waiting here in line," I said.

"Just give me a second to help these people and then I'll be right with you," Beth said. "Grab a seat."

I did as Beth asked and walked to the small table in the corner. I picked up the newspaper that lay on the table, one that someone had left behind. I absently scanned the headlines, although I didn't care. It didn't take very long before Beth arrived with my order, putting the three cups on top of the newspaper and sitting down next to me.

"I don't have very long, but I need to know what's going on. I won't be able to contain my curiosity if you walk out of here without telling me anything."

I laughed. "You're very invasive for someone who didn't want to go looking for Claire Whiteside with me," I said. Beth had told me that it was my mission and she wasn't going to join me on it.

"I wish I had!" Beth cried out. "Honestly, I just thought that it would be a dead end. These letters never amount to anything."

I nodded. It was true, usually when letters like these were found, it was impossible to track down the people involved. Stories like these, with Claire and Thomas both alive and where we could find them, were very, very rare.

"Well, Dane and I went to Montana to track Thomas down, you know that part," I said. I had told Beth when I had left so that she wouldn't come calling at the shop with coffee for me every morning.

"Did you share a room?" Beth asked, and she waggled her eyebrows.

"Stop it," I said with a giggle and a blush. Because obviously, I didn't even have to answer that question. Beth knew exactly how serious Dane and I were getting.

"You guys seem to be getting very close," Beth pointed out. "It's going in a good direction, right?"

I nodded. "It really is. I mean, we haven't really spoken about where this is going and what we are to each other, but I feel like in a way, we don't have to do. We're just on a different level."

"That's great, Amelia," Beth said. "You can't very often say something like that about someone. Guys usually have to have things labeled to know where they belong. But Dane has always been a little different, and I think you two might be the exception to the rule."

I smiled and nodded. We were the exception to a lot of different rules. I had never had a relationship with anyone the way it was with Dane. He was just so different. So kind and caring, and compassionate. And despite his difficulties, and the demons he was fighting, he managed to crawl out of his shell and connect with me.

"How did you find Thomas?" Beth asked. "It's a very common name, isn't it?"

"It is. But Dane's grandmother told us where Thomas had lived when they had spoken about being together after the war. With that clue, it was just a matter of searching from there."

"I still can't believe it. It's pretty damn lucky that you found him at all. Very few people stay in one place for their whole lives anymore."

I nodded. It was true. The fact that we had found Thomas at all was more than just luck. It was as if the universe wanted everything to work out, as if it, too, wanted to see how the story would end.

"So, now that he's here, what now?" Beth asked.

"Now we take him to meet Claire," I said.

"When?"

"Today," I said.

Beth's mouth dropped open. "I can't believe it! So soon? How did you manage to persuade him to come in the first place?"

I shook my head. I reached for my latte and took a sip. I wasn't going to be able to sit here, talking about all these things without having my drink.

"We didn't have to persuade him. When we went to visit him the first time, we told him why we were there and what we wanted to do. We gave him some time to think about it. The rest was all him. When Dane and I went back to the ranch to speak to him again, to see if he had made up his mind, his bags were already packed."

Beth kept shaking her head. "I'm still having trouble believing all of this. I mean, I know it's real. But it's also unlikely. Can you even imagine it? You managed to track both of them down and they want to see each other again?"

"Well, Thomas definitely does," I said. "I'm still not a hundred percent sure that Claire wants to see him. But Dane is convinced that it's going to work out. And no matter what happens from here, it's the right thing to do."

Beth nodded. "It really is the right thing to do. And now that you have come this far, it would be weird just to back out, anyway. I'm so excited for your sake! You have to tell me everything."

"Of course!" I said with a giggle. "There's no way I'm going to be able to keep this to myself, no matter which way it goes."

I took out my phone and checked the time. "I have to get back. We're still going to make breakfast before we head out there. And I'm sure that these are cold by now." I pulled the other two drinks closer to me.

"Just pop them in the microwave, no one will know the difference," Beth said.

I laughed and stood. Beth stood as well. She gave me a hug.

"I'm so glad that this is working out for you. And that you are so happy, Amelia. You deserve it. Really."

"Thank you," I said, and I meant it. Beth was such a good friend and it was so good to know that I had support in what I was doing. Not only with Claire and Thomas's story, but with Dane, too.

"Good luck!" Beth said before she headed back to the counter to fill more orders. I waved at her and left the store.

As I walked back to the apartment, the two coffees in my hands, excitement bubbled up inside me and I laughed out loud. It was still impossible to believe that we had gotten this far. And today was the day. Today we were going to take Thomas to see Claire. Today, we were going to write the last page of the story.

Chapter 19

Thomas
1945

GETTING HOME AFTER the war was harder than it seemed it should be. The war was technically over, but it was still almost impossible to get back home, and it took me a couple of months in London, trying to arrange to be able to leave the country.

It was as if everyone had been so eager to bring us into the country when the war had started, but now that we wanted to get home, they didn't care so much about what happened to us.

And having to stay in London for so long after I knew that Claire wasn't here anymore was pure torture.

I was holed up in a city where she was everywhere to me. No matter where I went, I could hear her voice or smell her scent or see her face. The memories were overwhelming, crashing all around me. They were almost worse than the nightmares from the war.

But Claire was gone. She was in love with another man, she belonged to someone else now. And I had to get her out of my head. The sooner I was able to leave the city, the better. The sooner I was home, the sooner I could stop thinking about her and start living my life again.

Or what was left of it.

Finally, I managed to arrange for my safe passage home. It was a flight from London to New York, and I would still have to travel quite far to get home. But I would do anything to be back on the ranch.

One morning, about a week before I was able to leave, I received a letter from my sister. After I had returned from the war, I had written her and given her an address where she could find me until I returned home. I told her that I was safe.

Now, when I ripped open the letter, it felt like I was being hit all over again.

My brother had fallen ill, my sister wrote. He could no longer look after the ranch and they really needed me at home to help.

What else was going to go wrong? How was I going to be able to get through all this?

I had no idea how I was going to be able to survive it, after everything I had been through. I was physically and emotionally wrecked from the war, heartbroken after losing Claire, and now I was going to have the responsibility of running the ranch alone. So much for going home to heal.

But a man had to stand up and do what needed to be done. And since I had nothing else to lose, working myself to the bone didn't seem like a half bad idea.

When I finally returned home, putting my feet back on American soil, I felt like I was going to collapse right there. I hadn't thought I would ever make it home again. When I had been in the middle of the fray, with bullets flying all around me, I had been sure that I would never see my family or the ranch again. And now, with my feet back on the land where I had been born, I wanted to fall to my knees and kiss it.

It still took me several days to get to Montana, to get back to the ranch.

Finally, when I stood at the end of the long driveway that led to the family house, I took a deep breath and let it out again, slowly. I wasn't the same man that had left this place, not even close. I was someone else now, merely an echo of who I had been. Would they even recognize me? Would they understand what it was like for me now? Would they try to get to know the person I had become?

But it was family. Of course, they would.

This was where I was wanted. This was where I was needed. And this was where I would stay. Because clearly, Claire hadn't wanted me enough to wait. She had promised, but too much time had passed. I had been the one on the front lines. I had been the one who had put my life in danger, taking bullets for my country, for the country of another. And for her. And she had thrown it back in my face without thinking about it twice.

How could she have cared so little?

I started walking to the farmhouse. I was still limping a little and the walk was far, but the exercise was good and I pushed myself harder. I didn't want to think about her. I didn't want to wonder about her anymore. I was so tired. I had spent the better part of the year in a city where she wasn't any more, knowing that she had left me. I promised myself that as soon as I was home, as soon as I walked into my family home, I wouldn't think of Claire again. She didn't deserve that from me. She hadn't deserved all the love I had given her, the promises I had made her.

It was so difficult to walk up to the ranch house, to see the porch where I had envisioned myself sitting with her, watching the sunset as husband and wife. Even back here at home, where she had never been, everything was tainted with the thoughts and the memories of her.

Dammit! I was so angry with what she had done to me. I was so upset with how she had shattered me.

I put one foot in front of the other, dragging my beaten body forward as I finally made it to the ranch house. I climbed the two steps onto the porch, walked to the door and knocked.

It was strange to knock on the front door of my own home, but it didn't seem right to just yank it open and storm inside.

When the door opened, my sister stood in front of me. She looked me up and down, her eyes filling with tears.

"Thomas! It's really you." She pulled me into a hug, holding me tightly. "I was so scared you would never come home again."

"I'm back, sis," I said. "And I'm not leaving ever again."

She held onto me for a while longer before she finally let go.

"Everyone else is in the kitchen," she said. "Come, sit down. You need to rest."

She had no idea. I didn't just need to rest my weary bones. I needed to rest my soul.

When I walked into the kitchen, it was as if I had never left. My sister sat down in her usual seat, next to her husband. My brother sat at the head of the table and when I saw him, I knew that he didn't have a lot of time left. He was very thin and had lost a lot of weight and muscle. His eyes were sunken with dark circles beneath them, and he looked frail and weak when he stood to hug me.

"Welcome home, brother," he said. His voice was hoarse. "We missed you so much."

"Well, none of that anymore," I said. I had to stay strong. I felt like I was going to collapse, but my brother was clearly very sick and my sister was worried. I could see it a mile away. There was no time for me to pity myself, or to lay down and die. I had to stand up and be the strong one.

I sat there talking to my brother, my sister and her husband. I wished that my parents were still here. I missed them so much.

Two kids ran into the kitchen, wailing about something.

"Well, who is this?" I said, turning around in my seat.

"This is Max and Sarah," my sister said, introducing me to my young niece and nephew.

I felt a pang in my chest. I had been gone so long, I had missed the birth of two children. My family.

"This is your Uncle Thomas," my sister said to them. "He's a hero."

I smiled at them as they said a quick hello and continue to play. I tried not to look sad. Because what my sister had said was wrong. I wasn't a hero. I wasn't anything but a shell of a man who was barely alive.

At least I still had people here who loved me. People who cared about me. And unlike Claire Whiteside, these people would never leave me. They would be here no matter what. They had stayed here all through the war, and they would be here forever after. Because that was what family was all about, wasn't it? It was sticking around through the hard times, keeping promises and being there for each other.

As the night dragged on, we caught up. My sister and brother explained to me what had happened at the ranch. There had been a terrible drought and we had lost a lot of cows. Then there had been floods when the rains finally started again, and a few more had drowned. The ranch had seen difficult times. But it had seen good times, too. In the years after the trouble, my brother and sister had managed to pick the ranch up again, making it flourish.

"At least it's not something impossible for you to pick up," my brother said. "We've managed to get the ranch back on its feet for you."

"For us," I said with a smile. "You guys did a brilliant job. When I walked up, I could see it looks great. I can't tell you how good it is to be home."

"What happened to you over there, Thomas?" My sister asked carefully. "I'm not talking about the war, either. Something about you seems different. You seem broken somehow."

I pulled up my shoulders and felt like crying. But I swallowed down the lump in my throat because men didn't cry.

"I guess war will do that to you," I said.

But I knew what my sister was seeing. She had always been extremely sharp, very in tune with my emotions. What she was seeing was my broken heart. She was seeing what Claire Whiteside had taken from me. But I wasn't going to tell them about Claire, I wasn't going to explain to them what had happened, and how I had fallen for a girl who ran away with my heart. That would only give her the acknowledgement she didn't deserve.

No, I wasn't going to keep her memory alive by speaking about her. I was going to continue with my life, living everyday as if she didn't exist at all. And if my brother and sister didn't know about her, they wouldn't ask.

"Are you sure that's all?" my sister asked.

I nodded. "It's impossible to explain how awful it was, sis. But with time, I'll get better again."

My sister reached for my hand and took it into hers.

"We are all here for you, Thomas. Always."

I nodded. "I know."

It was wonderful spending time with my family again. And having children in the house made it seem so much more alive. But no matter how good it felt to be back, no matter how much fun we had, it fell short somehow.

Because, I had dreamed about this reunion the entire time I was gone. I had imagined bringing Claire home with me, introducing her to my family. This night should have been with her at my side, my future wife.

I had never, not once in all the years I had been at war, envisioned coming back here alone. Not because something had happened to her, but because she had just decided that I wasn't worth the wait.

Chapter 20

Dane

I WOKE UP WITH SOMEONE kissing my face and judging by the perfume that surrounded me like a cloud, it was Amelia. Of course, it was Amelia. But it was Amelia in real life, it wasn't just a dream. I often dream about Amelia kissing me like that, waking up to her beautiful face.

"Good morning," she said, in a sultry voice with a soft smile.

"What time is it?" I asked, trying to look for my phone on the nightstand.

"It's still early, don't worry." She sat down next to me on the bed and I noticed that she was wearing my sweatshirt.

"What are you wearing?" I asked.

Amelia looked down and blushed. "I headed out to get coffee but I didn't have anything warm enough. I took the liberty to grab something out of the closet. I hope you don't mind."

I smiled, cupped her cheek with my hand and pulled her closer for a kiss. "Of course it's okay. Besides, I kind of like my clothes on you."

She smiled and it was such a beautiful thing. Everything about her was beautiful, but there were times that I was blown away by it, and taken off guard by how much she means to me.

"Do I smell coffee?" I asked, suddenly aware of the aroma in the room.

Amelia smiled and nodded. She reached behind her and produced a paper cup and a paper bag.

"What's this?" I asked.

"Breakfast."

When I sipped the cup, it was my favorite—hazelnut latte. And when I opened the bag, it was freshly baked bread.

"Did you go to the bakery?" I asked.

Amelia nodded. "I was going to just get coffee, but on the way back I couldn't resist. The bakery had just opened and the smell coming from inside was to die for. So I thought I would bring some home for us."

Home. I loved it when she said those words.

Amelia climbed under the covers with me again.

"I love that you are so comfortable in my apartment," I said. "But I have one problem."

"What?" Amelia asked, frowning.

"You're wearing too many clothes."

Amelia giggled and started stripping, sitting up so that she could get rid of the clothes. It wasn't necessarily that I wanted her again, although I always wanted her. Mostly, I just wanted to be close to her without clothes being in the way. I didn't know how to explain it, but having one-on-one time with her, naked in bed together, was something I cherished.

Besides, we were going to have to get up and dressed soon anyway. Today was the big day. The moment I thought about it, the reality hit me. We had come this far, and this was where the story would end. This was where we found out what would happen. Either this ending would be very happy, or it would be a tragic one.

"Where did you go?" Amelia asked. "You're suddenly distant."

"I was just thinking, and wondering how today would turn out," I said.

"You still think it might go wrong?" Amelia asked.

I shrugged my shoulders and took a bite of the bread. It crunched under my teeth and the taste was absolutely heavenly. I closed my eyes and chewed for a moment, focusing on nothing else. When I opened my eyes, Amelia was looking at me with an amused expression.

"I don't know," I finally said, answering her question. "I just keep thinking that we shouldn't get our hopes up. I'm worried that it might not be the happy ending we were hoping for, after all."

Amelia nodded. "I understand where you're coming from. But it's like we said in Montana. Even if Claire and Thomas never get to see the sunrise over those hills, it was enough that we were there. Right? I mean, look at what this journey has done for us. Look at how far we have come."

And of course, she was right. We had come so far and we had experienced so much together thanks to this story, to this journey. And it wasn't over yet, no matter what happened.

"I have to confess something to you," Amelia said.

"Yeah?" I asked. I was suddenly a little nervous. What could she possibly have to say to me? I was worried that it might be something bad, something that would ruin all of this. But as much as I racked my mind, trying to think of something that might be a bad thing, I just couldn't think of anything.

"Don't look so worried," Amelia giggled. "All I'm trying to tell you is that I've never felt so close to someone before."

I blinked at Amelia and relief flooded through me. It wasn't bad at all, and honestly, it was kind of ridiculous that I thought it might be.

I grinned at Amelia. "I know. I like Thomas, too."

Amelia laughed. "Very funny. You're such an ass, sometimes," she said. "Comic relief, right?"

I chuckled. That was exactly what I had been trying to do, to deflect how panicked I had suddenly felt. I realized just how much I liked Amelia, how much I didn't want to lose her. If she said something like that to me, I suddenly feared that she wouldn't be mine anymore. After all, she wasn't technically mine, not yet. We hadn't spoken about what we were to each other or how we felt.

"You know I was talking about you, right?" Amelia asked, when I didn't say anything. "I never expected you."

I smiled and pulled her closer for another kiss.

"I didn't really expect you, either. I mean, I thought I would be tending to my grandmother's roses in peace for the rest of my life."

Amelia giggled.

I kissed her again. Putting down the coffee I had been holding onto, the bread half forgotten. I pulled Amelia closer to me, hugging her tightly against me, pressing my lips against hers. I was never going to let go of this. I was never going to let her slip through my fingers the way Claire had slipped away from Thomas. It hadn't been his fault, of course. But I would never let anything take Amelia from me. She was the person I wanted to be with. She was the person that made me feel alive again after I'd been so worried that the man I had been had died.

Amelia was a breath of fresh air and I sort of saw her as my second lease on life. A chance to try again. A chance to realize that love could be for me, too.

"I know what you mean," I said to Amelia, my voice serious. I wasn't joking around anymore. "Since the moment you came along, everything changed. And I'm not talking about this journey we are on, either. My whole life has changed, thanks to you."

Amelia blushed. "You did most of the changing by yourself," she pointed out.

"But with you by my side to support me through it," I said. "And that's how I like it. You mean more to me than you realize."

Amelia looked like she didn't know what to say, so she kissed me instead. And that was perfect. Sometimes, words just didn't cut it.

I ran my hands over her body again. Everything about her was so soft and sensual. And I loved the way she felt under my hands.

We kissed and we touched each other and it was slow and sensual. Sometimes, there was so much passion between us that neither of us could contain it and we needed a release, right away. But sometimes, like now, everything was perfect. And I didn't want to rush through it, I didn't want to focus on the end result of what we were doing.

Right now, I wanted to focus on every inch of her body, and every second we spent together. I wanted to focus on the taste of her skin, the feel of her hands on my back and shoulders, the taste of her breath on my lips.

Her hair was soft when I stroked it and when I ran my fingers over her lips, she turned her face and kissed my fingers.

Everything about the way we were together was emotional. This wasn't fucking, this was making love.

When I was finally inside of her, it didn't feel like we were going through the motions, either. It never really felt that way with her, but this time was even more intense than any other time we had spent together. Amelia and I were more in tune than ever before. As I thrust into her, my body on top of hers, my chest pressing against her breasts, I looked into her eyes. Her green eyes were bright, her lids drooped a little and her lips were parted. She was so lost in the moment and I was right there with her.

We were in a bubble, removed from the rest of the world. Right now, nothing mattered other than us being together. And the way she felt underneath me, around me. The heat from her core translated to mine and when she orgasmed, I could feel the connection even though I hadn't myself.

We switched positions once or twice, but that wasn't what this was about. We weren't exploring. We weren't playing games. We were connecting with each other on a different level than we had before.

And if I thought at any point that we were falling for each other, this was the point of no return. There was no way I was going to be able to turn away from her now, to go back to a life without her. Amelia was stuck with me now. I wanted to be with her permanently. We fit together in a way I'd never come close to with another person.

In a way I had never thought possible.

At the end of it, I did have that orgasm. And so did Amelia. Twice actually. And it had been fantastic. But again, the orgasm, the sexual bliss wasn't what it had been about at all. This had been about Amelia and me, and what we were to each other and what we could become when we were together.

We lay next to each other on the bed, breathing hard, covered in sweat. We had to start getting ready soon. We had to go to my gran's place. We had to help Thomas find his lost love.

But right now, I didn't want to leave this room. I didn't want this moment to end. I wanted to stay in this bubble forever without allowing anything to break the spell. I wanted to be with Amelia, like this, for as long as I could have it.

And it looked like she felt the same way. She rolled onto her side and traced my face with her fingers. Her eyes slid over my features and her thoughts were racing. I could see it, and I wanted to know what she was thinking.

But a part of me already knew. Because I felt like I was thinking exactly the same thing.

But I didn't want to ruin anything, not by adding words to the mix, or attaching labels, or anything else. I just wanted to stay in this moment for as long as I could, with Amelia, this woman that had come to mean everything to me.

Chapter 21

Claire
1955

THE SUN WAS ALREADY above the horizon when I crept to the front door. I had been coming home later and later, pushing my luck. Every time, Reggie had still been asleep on the couch.

I knew I was taking chances, but what could go wrong? Reggie wouldn't realize if the house fell apart around him. He barely noticed anything anymore.

Carefully, I pushed open the door. Slipping inside, I put my shoes on the floor. I had crept up to the front door in my stockings, to be sure that I didn't make any noise. I reached into my pocket and slid my wedding ring onto my finger. I had nearly forgotten about that, too.

The house was quiet. Too quiet. I turned my head, listening, straining for a sound. Reggie's snoring didn't full the house the way it usually did. Maybe he had turned onto his side for a change, clearing up his airways. When he drank beer, he always got so blocked up. But the man never learned.

I picked up my shoes again and crept through the hall toward the bedroom. I wasn't even going to check the living room, since I knew what I was going to find. But as soon as I passed the door, the light in the living room flicked on. Reggie stood next to the couch, looking sober, bright, and fully dressed.

He didn't look anything like the man that always woke up groggy in the morning, hung over from drinking too much and smelling like old alcohol.

My throat constricted and my body ran cold. I had been caught.

"Where were you, Claire?" Reggie demanded. He didn't call me darling or dear. In all this time we had been so distant from each other, Reggie had still called me by pet names. It was as if it had come with the territory. But today, suddenly I was Claire.

At first, I wanted to cry. I wanted to plead guilty and ask for forgiveness. But anger overwhelmed me and took over.

"Why do you suddenly care about where I am?" I asked.

Why the hell was Reggie questioning me? What did he care, anyway? He had been ignoring me for months on end. There was a reason I had been going somewhere else to find a bit of attention.

I was so angry and ready for a fight. Typically, Reggie was ready for one too. They were days where it became a full on row. Especially when Junior wasn't home. Where was he right now? I realized with a shock that I didn't even know if my son was at home or not.

But I would worry about that later. Right now, I was going to take on my husband. He wasn't going to be able to push me into a corner on this one. Yes, I had been wrong. But it wasn't like Reggie had been right. Not in years.

Instead of fighting, though, Reggie shoulders slumped forward and he lowered himself wearily into his armchair. When I looked at him, I saw an old man, devoid of the arrogance of the man that I shared this house with. He lifted one hand, scrubbed his face and turned it away so I couldn't see his expression. All of this seemed like defeat.

I had never seen Reggie like this, and a pang of guilt stabbed into my chest.

"You're having an affair, aren't you?" Reggie asked, and his voice was hoarse. Was he going to cry? Was it possible that he actually cared?

It was difficult to believe. A man that cared didn't act the way he had for so long.

For a moment, I thought about lying. After all, it wasn't like Reggie deserved to know the truth, not with the way he had been treating me all this time. I could just say I'd gone out for a drink, gotten too drunk to come home and stayed at a hotel room or something.

But I couldn't lie to him. Reggie might have been a terrible husband, but I had done absolutely everything that made me a terrible wife. The betrayal was complete. I couldn't make it even worse by lying.

I took a couple of steps into the living room, aware that I wasn't wearing my shoes. It made me feel dirty, somehow. I should have been better dressed. I should have looked more put together. It was who I was supposed to be as Reggie's wife.

Then again, I was supposed to be a lot of things that I wasn't any more.

I sat down in a seat opposite Reggie.

"Yes," I finally admitted. "I'm having an affair."

Reggie sighed and it looked like the answer broke him, even though he must have already known the truth. Somehow, that made me feel even guiltier. How was it possible that someone who cared so little about me could be so affected by the news?

"How long?" Reggie asked. He looked worse and worse, as if the news was wearing him down in front of my eyes. His voice was so thick, now.

"A couple of months," I said.

Reggie looked up at me, shock registering on his face. "Months?"

What did he expect from me? Did he think it had only happened the one time? Had he thought I'd been happy? How could he not have noticed how far we had slipped?

"Three," I said flatly.

Reggie shook his head, looking toward the window and out at the roses. Those blasted roses. They had always gotten more of his attention than I had. I would never resent a flower, but, could Reggie not have thought for two seconds that he could put his attention elsewhere? Could he not have noticed me, at least for a moment?

"I knew things were bad between us, Claire," Reggie said, still not looking at me. When he spoke, it sounded like a sigh. "But I never thought, I never dreamed you would do such a thing." He took another deep breath. "How could you do this to me?"

I didn't know how he could even ask me that question. Had he not been living in this house? Did he not know what we had been through? How bad things had gotten? How many times had I asked him for things to be different? How many times had I told him that I wasn't happy? At first, many times. But as time passed and he had ignored my pleas, I'd eventually stopped saying it.

And now? I couldn't say that it was his fault. But I wasn't the only one that had driven me to this point.

"Let's be honest, Reggie," I said, finally speaking. "I don't really know you anymore. Who are you? When we got married, we were practically strangers. But over the years that hasn't changed. How much effort have we put in to get to know each other? How much time have you paid attention to me?"

"Dammit, Claire!" Reggie cried out and stood, walking to the far window. He was so angry I could see it radiating off of him. "Don't make it sound like I drove you to this."

"We walk around this house like strangers, you and I. What are we supposed to do? How am I supposed to save something if I'm the only one fighting for it?"

"I'm not listening to this," Reggie said, shaking his head. He walked out of the living room. But I wasn't having any of it.

"Oh, no, you don't," I said, getting up and storming after him. "You don't get to decide when this conversation is over. If you didn't end at least half of our conversations, maybe we would have gotten somewhere. Maybe I would have felt the liberty to speak to you about certain things."

I was brimming with emotion, and didn't know how to hold back my anger, my bitterness, or my sorrow. But Reggie didn't seem to feel the same. Anger crackled between us, but aside from that, he just seemed tired.

When we reached the bedroom, he spun around and glared at me.

"I know that I'm not perfect, and that our relationship isn't what it should be. Do you think that I don't? I've seen how happily my friends are married and wished that I had that. But you're not exactly happy either, are you? I'm not the man of your dreams. We've established that before."

"And we said we were going to make a difference, that we were going to change it," I retorted. "We said we were going to try to be better for each other."

"I tried!" Reggie shouted. "I did what you wanted me to do. I was there when you needed me, I paid attention to you when I came home. I spoke to you and asked about your day."

"But you wouldn't stand up for me when I needed you to," I said. "You keep letting your family trample me. You don't stand by my side as if we are a team. You allow them to disgrace me."

Reggie shook his head. "My family has been nothing but kind to you. We gave you a home when you were lost in the war."

"Don't you dare bring that up," I said. "You know that my father arranged this. It wasn't me begging you to take me along."

"If I had known that your father was talking such bullshit when he said you would be the perfect housewife, I would never have married you in the first place."

Even though I hadn't wanted to marry Reggie, even though I didn't love him, his words still stung.

"I tried," I said in a small voice. "I tried for you, Reggie. I did everything you wanted, and tried to do everything your mom told me to do.

I was never good enough for you, was I? Because I'm not an American girl and I never will be."

Reggie waved his hand at me. "This isn't about that."

"Then what is it about?" I asked. "You've mentioned before that you'd rather have an American girl, right? At the end of the day, I'm just not what you want. And I never will be. Why are you so upset if someone else wants me?"

"Because you're supposed to be at home!" Reggie shouted.

"To cook and clean for you? To make sure you have a house to come home to that is exactly the way you want it to be? All you want is a domestic worker. You don't want a wife."

Reggie planted his hands on his hips and shook his head, turning away from me. This fight was going nowhere and I knew it. But I was finally able to say everything I felt. Reggie and I were finally talking. How long had taken to get to this point? And why could we only have a conversation when we fought?

"You didn't have to go and look for someone else. You didn't have to throw me away like that," Reggie said. The fight had left his voice, but I wasn't done yet.

"Don't you dare," I said. "Don't you dare turn me into the villain. All I wanted was for someone to hold me. To fucking touch me, Reggie. To make me feel like I'm alive."

Reggie looked at me and in his face, I saw the eyes of a broken man. Again, the guilt shot through my chest, but I pushed it away. Why was it wrong of me to want something? Why was it wrong to need something that should have been normal in a marriage? I wasn't going to allow him to make me feel like I was the one that was wrong. Not when he had been just as bad.

We had both been wrong in this case. In different ways, perhaps, but neither of us was innocent.

Reggie sank down onto the bed, dropping his head into his hands. He sat like that for the longest time and I tried my best to hold onto my anger, to not let it slip away leaving only the guilt behind.

"There is one thing you don't seem to understand," Reggie finally said in a whisper. "You don't seem to realize that I want that, too."

Chapter 22

Thomas
Present Day

I STOOD IN FRONT OF the mirror, looking at myself. I'd been awake since the crack of dawn this morning and heard the kids talking in the room next door. I figured they weren't ready to get up just yet, and I understood. I'd been young once upon a time, too. They had seemed to find a genuine love and they deserved to celebrate it.

Besides, it was still far too early to see Claire. So, I had stayed in bed, trying to read a book I had brought along.

But I hadn't been able to concentrate. Today, everything would change for me. No matter what happened when we went to visit Claire, I would finally have my answers.

After what felt like forever, Amelia called me to breakfast. She had bought me coffee and freshly baked bread which was far better than anything I had ever tasted at the ranch. Dane had offered me butter and I'd spread it on the bread, watching it melt. They must have warmed up the bread again, but it was as if it had come fresh out of the oven.

"How are you feeling?" Amelia asked while I ate.

"Nervous," I said. "I don't know what to expect."

"There's only one way to get past that," Dane said.

I nodded. I took another bite of the bread and chewed, thinking. The only way to deal with anything was to close my eyes and jump. I had known that for the longest time.

Seeking a distraction, I occupied myself by watching Dane and Amelia. They moved around the kitchen as if they were completely in sync. And when they stole little glances at each other, sure that I wasn't watching, they shared secret smiles. I didn't know what had happened between them since yesterday afternoon, but it was almost as if they were closer than ever. It made me so happy inside.

When I had finished my coffee and bread, Dane asked if I wanted to shower. I nodded and headed to the bathroom with my toiletry bag, the nerves returning now that there was nothing to distract me.

After taking a shower, trimming my beard and making sure that I looked as put together as I could, I went back to the guestroom and took out the clothes I had decided to wear to meet Claire.

I didn't have much in the way of fancy clothes. I was just a farmer, after all. But I had packed my nicest flannel shirt and jeans, and heavy duty shoes rather than the boots I usually wore. And I hadn't brought the hat along with me. That was saying something. The man Claire was going to see today was as good as it was going to get.

When I had met her in that bar, I had been wearing my uniform. I had known I looked good in it, since I'd seen how women looked at us when we walked past. Was Claire going to accept the person I was now? She had never seen me like this.

Then again, she had never seen anything about me like this. Not the clothing and not the man inside it. I had changed so much after the war, everything that had made me the person I had once been was gone. When I met Claire, I'd been just a boy. Now? I was an old man with a life of regret behind him.

"Are you ready?" Dane asked, speaking from the other side of the door after knocking.

"As ready as ever be," I answered, and walked to the door.

We climbed into Dane's truck. I quite liked it, since it reminded me a little of the truck I used to drive when I was younger. It was down to earth, simple. This part of him I understood, and once again, I felt like I could relate to him.

The drive out of town didn't take very long, it was much shorter than I would have liked, and before I knew it, we were parked at the curb outside a large house.

I looked up at the home. It was really more of a mansion. With beautiful gardens wrapping around it. This place screamed money. Maybe not as much money as it could be, but this was definitely a lot better than anything I had ever been able to offer.

"It's beautiful," I said.

Dane nodded. "Yes, but it looks a lot nicer from the street than on the inside."

I frowned at Dane.

"Inside is nice," Amelia noted.

Dane shook his head. "That's not what I meant," he muttered.

Maybe Dane was just as nervous as I was. Did that mean I had reason to worry? I hoped not. We walked up the path to the front door. I wondered why Dane hadn't driven us up the drive. But maybe he had a reason. As we neared the house, my palms started sweating and my fingers trembled. My throat felt like it was swelling shut. I was so nervous, I couldn't even breathe. I was so glad I had these two kids with me. I would never have had the stones to do this alone. Hell, I wouldn't even have gotten as far as the gate of my ranch if it had been up to me alone.

As soon as we reached the front door, I hesitated. How had it happened that I had come here? How could it be that we had come this far?

"It all feels so surreal," I said. Because as soon as I lifted my fist and knocked on the door, Claire Whiteside would appear before me. And it felt like a dream. How long had I thought about something like this? Running into her, imagining what I would say?

"How is this happening?" I asked, but it was a rhetorical question. I didn't really expect either of the kids to answer me.

Amelia stood closer to me and placed her hand on my shoulder.

"Everything is going to be fine," she said. "All you have to do is knock."

She was right. I just had to lift my hand and knock on the door, I just had to take this last step. But this step seemed like the biggest step of all. Fifty years had passed. Five decades believing that Claire didn't want me, that she had chosen someone else. How many years had I spent resenting her, bitter about what she had done to me? How many years had I regretted meeting her at all?

Now that Dane had told me what Claire had shared with him, it was all different. But that didn't change the fact that I had been upset about it for so very long.

Was I going to be able to see her as the same woman? Was I going to be able to go back to before, when I hadn't thought of her as the villain who had wrecked my life?

There was so much to be afraid of. Not just how I felt about her, but about how she might feel about me. What if she didn't want me? Or worse, what if she didn't remember me? I didn't know which would be worse.

"Thomas," Dane said gently. "It's going to be okay. No matter what happens. Remember, this is where you finally get your answers."

And of course, he was right. They both were. And I had agreed to come with them for a reason. I couldn't back out of it now.

Finally, I lifted my hand and wrapped my knuckles on the door. For a moment, everything was silent. And then a faint voice called out from the inside that they were coming.

My pulse fluttered and I felt lightheaded. I would know that voice anywhere. In a crowd with a million voices, I would still be able to pick out which one belonged to her. Even now, with a slight waver of age.

We waited for what felt like forever. It was probably only a few seconds, but time seemed to stretch out into infinity.

And then, finally, the door swung open. And there she stood in front of me. She smiled as she turned to the familiar face first. Dane, her grandson. And then she looked at Amelia, her face changing a little bit, her eyes losing the smile that was still plastered on her face. And oh, how beautiful she was. Her hair was great, but her eyes were as dark and captivating as ever. And her face, so regal, so beautiful. She may have aged, but Claire was still exactly the same.

Finally, she turned her eyes to me. She stared silently at me and I stared back at her.

"Claire," I breathed, finally breaking the silence.

She still stared at me, blinking. And then there was recognition in her eyes. "Thomas?" she asked.

I nodded and pressed both hands to my chest. "Yes. It's me."

A myriad of emotions flickered over her face and I couldn't read any of them. They were there and then gone again so quick. She slammed down the wall, her eyes guarded and her face expressionless. She turned back to Dane.

"What is this?" she asked.

Dane opened his mouth to answer, but Claire shook her head.

"I thought I told you not to do this to me."

She took a step back and slammed the door shut. I stared at it in shock. My ears rang. Just like that, like a vision, Claire had appeared, and now she was gone again. My body felt like lead. Of all the things I had imagined, of all the ways I had pictured this going down in my mind, this reaction hadn't been one of them. I hadn't thought that she might not even want to see me at all, that she didn't even want to speak to me. She had only said one word to me.

"So, that's that, then," I said.

Because it was quite clear what was going on. She had slammed the door shut in my face after taking one look at me. Her emotions had been clear. Claire Whiteside wanted nothing to do with me. After all this time, I had been right.

When I found out that she had come to America with another man, I had been furious that she had fallen in love and moved on. I had been enraged that she had what it took to get over me when it had taken me a lifetime to try and just forget her, let alone erase how I felt about her. But now, standing here, having experienced her wrath, I finally understood that even though she might have been told to do so by her father, she had still done that one thing.

She had moved on.

The knowledge hit me in the chest like a physical punch and I staggered backward. Dane and Amelia both grabbed for me, trying to stop me from falling. They helped me gain my balance again, to stand on my own two feet. But even though I wasn't as frail as I had been a second before, I still felt like a part of me had been shattered.

Why had I come here? Why had I gotten my hopes up at all? I realized that I had believed it would go so differently. I had expected something, even though I told myself not to. And now? I was the one that had been hurt again. I was the one standing here, alone with a broken heart. Again.

Chapter 23

Dane

I STARED AT THE FRONT door my grandmother had just slammed shut and I could feel the shock radiating from Thomas. It mirrored my own. Of all the scenarios I had pictured for today, this hadn't been one of them.

"Dane," Amelia said in a breathy voice, looking at me with wide eyes. She had been caught off guard as well.

We both looked at Thomas. He stood there, staring at the door, his face a mask of horror and pain. What had this been like for him? He had come all this way with so much hope. We had given him so much to look forward to. And now my gran had been a downright bitch about it.

I knew that was rude, but how could she react like this? This wasn't right. The least she could do after what she had done to Thomas was to give him a chance. After all, she had left without even letting him know what was happening. I knew that it wasn't her fault, that her father had made her do it. She had explained everything to me.

But what she could do was explain everything to Thomas, too. At least that, if nothing else.

"This isn't over, Thomas," I said, putting my hand on the old man's shoulder.

Thomas started shaking his head, but I wasn't going to take no for an answer. This wasn't going to be how this story ended. I pushed the door open, walking into the house without knocking again. I left Thomas standing there.

Amelia tried to follow me but I turned around and shook my head.

"You have to stay here, with Thomas," I said.

"Why?" she asked, and she looked disappointed.

"I think it's best to let me talk to her alone."

Amelia opened her mouth to argue, but then she closed it again and nodded. She wasn't going to argue with me, but I knew that she was disappointed and I would have to explain it to her, later. And I would.

But right now, I had to deal with my gran. She was fickle and she didn't trust easily. And then there was her entire past and everything she was trying to bury. Everything she was trying to push away as if it had never happened. But it wasn't possible to live a life like that. If anyone knew that it was impossible to ignore something, it was me.

I just had to do this alone.

Amelia stayed behind with Thomas as I closed the door again, closing myself in the house with my grandmother. I walked through the rooms, going to look for her. Eventually, I found her in the sitting room at the back of the house. She stood by the window, looking out over the garden.

"Nanna," I said.

My gran didn't look at me. She just covered her eyes with a shaking hand.

"Please leave, Dane," she said.

"No," I said with a gentle voice. "Please hear me out."

She sank down into an armchair close by and dropped her head into her hand. She looked so small and frail like this, ridden with emotion. She usually sat upright and proud, able to handle anything she felt. But it was impossible to stay strong all the time. Even for her.

I walked over and crouched down in front of her so I could look her in the eye.

"I didn't do this to you, Nanna. I did this *for* you. Neither of you have ever had the chance to get answers. Why not take this opportunity to make peace with the past? Or to look at the man you used to love, to touch him, hold him, feel that he is real. That he's alive."

As I spoke, her face crumpled and it looked like she was going to give in. But then she sat up, her back stiff and her eyes sharp when she looked at me. There wasn't a single trace of the tear. Her lips were pursed together.

"Why on earth would I need to do that?" she snapped.

I took a deep breath and let it out slowly. "Because it's what I needed to do, Nanna. Reaching for her hands, taking both of them in both of mine, I took a deep breath. "When I saw you for the first time after the shooting, I had to make sure that everything I saw, everything I touched, was real. I didn't think I would ever see you again. When I was lying on that floor bleeding out, I was sure it was the end. So being able to hold you and know that I still had time with you was worth every moment of suffering. You deserve that, too. He deserves to be able to look back and know that it wasn't all bad. You both deserve to get your answers, and to be happy again."

My grandmother looked at me for a long time and I hoped that she was considering my words.

But she shook her head. This time, I could see her fighting off the tears. I had never seen my grandmother fall apart. I had never seen her be so emotional. She had always been the backbone in our family, the one to stand strong when everyone else faltered.

"What's wrong, Nanna?" I asked when she didn't speak. "Why don't you just tell me what's going on in your mind?"

A tear rolled over her cheek. I had never, ever seen my gran cry.

"I don't deserve it, Dane," she said in a whisper.

I shook my head. "No, everyone deserves a second chance."

"Just listen," my Gran said. "I'm a bad person, Dane. I don't do good things. I do wicked things. I hurt people."

I shook my head again. I just wasn't willing to believe that about her. My gran had always been the most pure and beautiful person I had ever known. She had always done everything expected of her, always stood up and put one foot in front of the other, even though there were so many times she could have laid down and given up. Even after my grandfather died, my gran had continued on with her head held high.

Even though I now knew that she had never loved my grandfather, it didn't mean that it was easy to lose him. I knew that. But she had done everything in her power to make sure that everyone else was okay, to carry on through the hard times. I wanted to do that for her, now. She needed that.

"No one is bad, Nanna," I said.

"I am," my gran said. She looked down at our hands, still together. "I abandoned him. Don't you understand that? I promised him that I would wait. Thomas was out there, sacrificing his life. Who knows what horrors he has seen. I promised him I would be there when he came back. But I wasn't. Do you know what that must have done to him? There isn't a day in my life that I don't feel haunted by how much I hurt him. I abandoned Thomas, Dane. He needed me when the war was over and I wasn't there. I was here. With Reggie." She twisted her face and looked disgusted. "Useless, boring, parent pleasing Reggie. Sexist, simple, easy. He was weak. And I had chosen him over Thomas. What does that say about me?"

I kept shaking my head as my gran spoke. "You didn't have a choice. You told me what happened. Your father sent you."

My gran nodded. "You're right. He did send me. I didn't exactly have a say in the matter. But I had a secret, Dane. A secret that I didn't tell anyone about. And that's the same as lying and betraying, isn't it? I did things."

I frowned. My gran kept saying she had done things, and that she was a bad person. That she should have done things differently. But I didn't know what she was talking about. I didn't know what she was referring to. And the more she said it, the more I started wondering if she really had done something she shouldn't have.

"What are you talking about, Nanna?" I finally asked. "What did you do?"

My gran took a deep breath and let it out slowly. She turned her head to the window again, and pulled her hands out of mine.

"Thomas was my first love. When I met him, I knew that I wanted to be with him for the rest of my life. And I gave myself to him. Completely, fully. You understand what I mean?"

I nodded. I understood what she was trying to say to me. Back in those days, sleeping together before marriage was a sort of scandal. I understood that. But I also understood what it was to love someone so much you couldn't breathe sometimes. So much that it became an ache in your bones. Sometimes, that was how I felt about Amelia. And I knew what it was to need to connect in a way that nothing else could cover. It was why I had slept with Amelia after our first date, even though I didn't usually do things like that.

Not with that much emotion and passion.

"You see, by the time I met Reggie, I had already given myself to someone else. I wasn't pure anymore. But I didn't tell him that. I didn't tell anyone. Because it wasn't just that my father wanted to get me out of the country, and wanted me to be taken care of. I had a reason to go. I didn't fight against it as hard as I should have."

I shook my head, still not understanding what she was trying to tell me.

"To want to be safe, to want to survive, is not a crime, Nanna," I said. "It must have been dreadful for you during the war, and not even knowing if Thomas was alive."

"But I wasn't just looking out for myself anymore, Dane," Gran said. "It wasn't just me that I was trying to keep safe anymore. Because by the time I met Reggie, I was with child."

I blinked, trying to understand what she was saying to me. I understood the words, but somehow, it didn't make sense.

"I didn't tell Reggie, so he assumed the baby was his. It was soon enough after I fell pregnant. Everything worked out perfectly and no one asked any questions, no one at all. And seeing that I was married, there was no scandal to cover up. There was no reason to say anything at all."

I felt like the truth was being moved from underneath me. Like someone was pulling out a giant rug.

"Nanna, are you saying—"

She looked at me and her eyes were full of tears again. They were so dark, so full of emotion. She took my hands again and squeezes them, tightly.

"Dane, Reggie isn't your grandfather. Thomas is."

I sat back, my ass flat on the floor. I couldn't believe what I was hearing. I couldn't believe what my gran was telling me. There was so much about my past, so much about who I was, that was very different than I had always believed. And gramps? The man I had called my grandfather my whole life? It turns out that he wasn't.

"That changes everything, doesn't it?" I finally said, sounding a little dazed.

My gran nodded. "It does."

Chapter 24

Claire

Present Day

I watched Dane's face as I told him that Thomas was his grandfather, not Reggie. It felt like an immense weight off my shoulders to finally admit what I had done. I had never told anyone about the baby, never told anyone that it wasn't Reggie's. I had kept the secret for over fifty years. And it had been such a heavy burden to bear for so very long.

But even though it felt good to finally tell someone, someone that might not judge me, I looked at Dane and I wasn't sure what he was thinking. He looked shocked, that was for sure. He had dropped from his heels that he had been sitting on, onto the floor. He had looked stunned, shocked. But now, his face was carefully expressionless.

I had no idea what he was thinking or feeling. And it made me unsure. I was an old woman, I had lived a long life. I could do whatever I wanted now, no one could tell me who I should be and what I should do any more. But still, I didn't want Dane to judge me. I wanted him to look up to me and still see the woman he had before.

Had I completely shattered his perception of me?

When he didn't say anything, I continued talking just to fill the silence. To try to get rid of the nerves that were building fast.

"Your father grew up believing the wrong man was his father," I said. "And I let him believe it. I let Reggie believe it, too." I took a deep breath. I kept feeling like I couldn't breathe, like my throat was tightening, like something squeezed my chest. I took one deep breath after the other but it didn't make a difference. How could telling a secret and feeling so light come with the same feelings of condemnation?

"I am a bad person, Dane." I had said that so many times, I was sure he was getting sick of hearing it. Or maybe he would finally believe me now. Because what kind of woman did that to someone? What kind of woman told one man that another man's baby was his? And it was the only child I ever had. Reggie's bloodline had died with him, and he hadn't even known it.

Dane still didn't say anything.

"I've taken my anger out on the wrong people," I said. I could see that clearly now. Hindsight was always perfect. "I lied. I manipulated, I cheated—"

"Nanna, stop," Dane said, cutting her off. "That's enough."

I was surprised that he was taking that tone with me, putting his foot down. But I closed my mouth, staring at him.

"You're not a bad person. I don't believe it. And it doesn't matter what you tell me, I still won't. I love you, and you are a part of me. And I know you've never been happy."

I wanted to burst out in tears. Of all the things I had expected to happen when I finally told someone my horrible secret, compassion and love hadn't ever been among the reactions I'd envisioned.

Dane reached for me and squeezed my hand. His touch was warm, caring, and loving. He really meant it when he said that he didn't think I was a bad person. How was that possible?

"Please," he said. "Come see Thomas. Let him inside."

He was going on about it again. I closed my eyes for a moment. I didn't know if I had what it took to do it. I didn't know if I could look Thomas in the eye after what I had done to him.

"I know this is hard, Nanna," Dane said. "But you've both been missing each other for decades. You can't keep punishing yourself for the things in the past. It's not going to serve you anymore. You've got to move on. You still have time."

When I looked at Dane, spewing so much wisdom, I looked at the man who had grown and matured beyond his years. Months ago, before the shooting had happened, he had been just a boy in so many ways, still. But the shooting had taken so much out of him and he had grown up as a result. He had learned how to deal with grief and pain and sorrow. He had learned how to recreate himself when everything about him had been ripped away. And what emerged was a man with a different kind of character. Stronger, wiser. And it showed.

And when he sat in front of me like this, talking to me about how it was time for me to look forward, instead of looking back all the time, I saw a man that was really preaching the words he had to follow himself.

"You have grown up, my boy," I said to him.

Dane looked surprised.

"I mean it. In front of me sits a man, very different from the person you used to be. You have so much wisdom and compassion to share with the world. But it would be a good idea for you to follow your own advice."

Dane frowned and shook his head, still looking unsure.

I smiled. "You can't control how things ended up in the shootout. I know that you blame yourself for Drew's death. I know that it still haunts you, every day. But you did everything that you were trained to do and you put yourself in the line of fire to save others. You are noble and you were brave. There was nothing you could have done to save Drew."

Dane's face crumpled when I said it. Because he knew that I was speaking the truth. And I knew that he had been beating himself up over his friend's death for months. I also knew what it was like to blame yourself for something that you couldn't have changed. In a way, it had been the same with Thomas.

I could see Dane fighting back his emotions. This hadn't been about him, he hadn't prepared to suddenly revisit things that he had been through. And I felt a little sorry that I had pushed him into that now. But the words he had said to me were words that he needed to hear, too.

"It's time to look forward, Dane," I said. "I guess you and I have the same lesson to learn, don't we? We need to learn to let go of the things in the past that weigh us down, and hold us back. Sometimes so many things can happen that prevent us from looking toward the future. And it's so easy to get caught up, to become bitter and stop seeing the beauty all around us."

Dane nodded. "That's how I felt for a long time. But things are changing, now. This story with you and Thomas. And Amelia."

I smiled at Dane. "I know that you feel a lot for her. And she's a darling girl."

Dane smirked at me. "Even though she intrudes and brings you letters you don't like?"

I laughed, rolling my eyes. "You know that has nothing to do with anything. The two of you caught me completely off guard with that. And you couldn't have known everything that I had been struggling with at the time.

Dane nodded. "I know, but I'm still sorry that we sprung it on you like that."

"Tell me about Amelia," I said. "I like the way your face lights up when you speak about her."

Dane offered me a shy smile. "I don't know what it is about her. But when she's with me, everything just feels different. It feels like... I don't know how to explain it."

"Like the world has color again," I said.

"Exactly," Dane said, nodding.

"That's how I felt when I met Thomas," I said. "That kind of love is rare. You don't find that kind of thing every day. Hell, you don't find that kind of thing in a hundred years. Trust me, I've seen a lot in my lifetime. I have lived a loveless life and seen my friends, the women I met here in America after getting married to Reggie, live much the same way. Even though they had loved their husbands in the beginning, it had died out. Because the kind of love that you and I are capable of feeling—the fiery love that will never burn out—it's rare and something that most people don't get to experience. And the moment you find it, you don't let go."

"I don't intend to," Dane said. "It's still early for us, Amelia and I didn't meet very long ago. But sometimes it feels like I have known her forever. And I know that I want her to be a part of my life far, far into the future."

I nodded. I was so glad to hear that Dane had found love. And that it was the kind of love that was worth fighting for, worth dying for. So few people really got to experience it, and that was a tragedy. But Dane seemed to know what he had and he wasn't going to let it go. He was such a good man. Despite his father turning out like Reggie, Dane had risen up and become so much more. I had always known that I liked him the best.

Dane stood up. "Well, now that you and I know that we are on the same page, that we know the past belongs in the past and the only thing we can do is look to the future, what do you say? Are we going to give this one more shot?"

Right, we were back to me. That was what this was all about, wasn't it? I could change the topic and throw it back onto Dane. I could talk to him about his love and I could distract him with words of wisdom about his past. But ultimately, Dane was here because he had brought Thomas home to me. And he wasn't going to forget about it.

I took a deep breath. "I'm terrified." It was the first time in my life I'd admitted it. Because the truth was, I was so scared to look Thomas in the eye after everything I had done to him.

"He wants to see you, Nanna. He's excited. He's missed you just as much as you've missed him. Give him a chance. See what happens between the two of you. At the very worst, you could find some answers and you too can part ways again. Anything on top of that is a bonus."

Of course Dane was right. He had been right about many things the past couple of weeks. But that didn't change how scary this was.

Dane held his hand out to me.

"Come, Nanna. I think it's time."

I took his hand and he helped me up. When I stood, I wavered. Dane put his arm around my shoulders, supporting me.

"It's going to be okay," he said. And when he said it like that, I was inclined to believe him.

"We are just going to put one foot in front of the other, and together, we are going to walk to the door. We are going to look forward, to the future. No more looking back for you and I, Gran. This is where we start living again."

His words hit me hard when he said that. How right he was. It was time to look forward. It was time to let go of the past. And maybe, just maybe, there was still a future to be had.

Slowly, we walked to the door. I took a deep breath before Dane reached for the handle and opened the door.

Chapter 25

Amelia

THE SUN WAS STARTING to sink behind the horizon. The sky was painted with splashes of orange and purple, and everything in Pinewood had been touched by a deep, rosy hue. As the day started to retreat, the night already in the air, Dane and I sat quietly in his truck.

We were still parked against the curb in front of Claire's house. We were waiting for Thomas, ready to take him home the moment he came out of the house, ready to be there for him in any way that he needed us.

But Thomas had gone into that house hours ago, and he still hadn't come out.

"If he hasn't come out yet, I think they hit it off," I said to Dane.

He looked at me and smiled. "I was thinking the same thing."

"I have a feeling he might not be staying with you tonight," I said with a grin.

Dane chuckled and nodded. "And that's our cue to get the hell out of Dodge."

He started the truck and it rumbled into the night air. Dane pulled into the road and slowly, we drove into Pinewood. As we drove, he put his hand on my knee.

"I can't believe this has actually happened," he said. "It's been such a long journey, with so many ups and downs, but it looks like we got our happy ending, after all."

I nodded and put my hand on top of his. "Against all odds, we did. Can you believe that all of this started with a simple letter at the bottom of a box? I still think that it's incredible that we found both of them, and both of them were still alive. And that they have the opportunity to be together again."

Dane nodded and we drove on in silence for a while.

He cleared his throat and glanced toward me. "I'm sorry I didn't invite you inside back there. I needed to have a private conversation with my Gran."

I smiled at him and nodded. "I know. I shouldn't have let it bother me. I understand."

Dane glanced at me again, curious. "Why did it bother you, though?"

I pulled up my shoulders. "I've just been a part of every step of the process until now. In fact, I was the one that wanted to find Claire in the first place. I mean, you weren't even interested in history when I met you. So I felt like this was my baby, you know? It was my project. And even though it became ours, I still felt like it was at least half mine. I didn't expect to be shut out of the final moment."

Dane nodded. "I understand. And that final moment with Thomas meeting my gran was a big one."

"But I do know why you did what you did," I added. "And you were right. I shouldn't have been there for that talk. I mean, I'm sure it was a special moment for you and your grandmother to have. This really is such a big thing, and we can't just storm through it without taking emotions into account."

"That's just the thing, Amelia," Dane said. "You have been part of each and every step. That moment was more about me and her than about her and Thomas."

"Oh?" I asked.

Dane nodded and stopped at the stop sign, looking both ways before crossing. We were getting closer to his apartment.

"We were talking about my grandmother's past, about why she didn't think she was worthy to see Thomas. And that sort of became about my past, too. We were connecting in ways that we never had before, and it was a moment we would never have had if we hadn't been alone."

"I'm so glad that you had that moment, then," I said. Sometimes, it wasn't possible to be there for everything. And even though I was dying with curiosity about everything they had talked about, I knew that there were times that things needed to stay private. After all, this wasn't just a love story to Dane, or a little bit of history that was interesting. To him, this was the history of his family. It was extremely personal.

I knew the people involved now, and it had become a little more personal to me in the process, but it would never be to me what it was to Dane.

"I can't tell you how much I appreciate your understanding in this, and how you've been by my side, supporting me every step of the way. In fact, I'm so glad that you made me a part of this journey. You easily could have kept the whole thing to yourself."

"I didn't want to," I said. "After that first date, I felt so comfortable with you I suddenly wanted to share every part of my life with you. I still do."

Dane nodded. "I feel the same way. You have no idea how serious I've become about you and everything we do together."

We drove for a short while longer in silence.

"Will you pull over?" I suddenly asked.

"We're almost at the apartment," Dane said.

"Please?" I asked.

Dane did as I asked, pulling to the side of the road and turning off the engine.

"Is everything okay?" he asked.

"More than okay," I said. I undid my seatbelt and clambered across the stick shift, climbing into Dane's lap. It was a little rough, and I stumbled twice, but when I landed in his lap, I was giggling and he had a big grin on his face.

"You really are something special, Amelia," he said, and ran his hand through my hair.

I planted a big kiss on his lips.

"I've been waiting for the right time to tell you this," I said. "I've been wanting to tell you this for a while."

Dane suddenly looked a little uncertain.

"And after what you just said," I continued, "I can't think of a better time than now. I love you."

Dane looked at me, surprised for a moment, but then his face softened. He wrapped his arms around me, pulling me closer, and gazed up at me.

"I didn't know when to tell you, either. But I love you, too."

He kissed me, and the moment was perfect. I would never have thought that I could fall for someone so quickly and so deeply. I had never told anyone that I loved them so soon into the game. But with Dane, everything was different. Since the moment I had met him, it felt like we fit together like puzzle pieces. His life and my life had been meant to collide. And from the moment we had gone on our first date, I had known that this was the man I wanted to be with. Everything with him was just incredible. And the more time I spent with him, the more I felt that way.

The trip to Montana had just proven to me that this was how it should be. Being with Dane was fate.

Everything else that we had been through, the love story, the letter, finding Claire and finding Thomas and finally bringing them together, it was all secondary to the love that grew between us. But it had definitely been a part of our journey. And this moment had been created because of it.

Everything about this, the bond formed between Dane and his grandmother, and the friendship we had started building with Thomas, it was something to be cherished. It was special. And it was so very rare. Not just our love, our relationship, the connection that pulled us together, but the love and affection between Thomas and Claire that had transcended decades.

This was the kind of love worth fighting for. The kind of love worth crossing oceans for, the kind of love worth dying for. And I was going to do everything in my power to make it work with Dane. Because you didn't find something like this every day and if the story with Thomas and Claire had taught me anything, it was that you didn't let go of something as precious as this when you found it.

I knew that they felt the same way. Not just about me, but about our relationship and how important it was to fight for our love. And that was exactly why everything between us was going to work out. Because we were two people who were perfect together, and we knew exactly what it meant to have to work hard to make it happen. Because love, as beautiful and as important as it was, could easily disappear if you didn't work at it.

But I was going to put in the effort every day. And I knew that Dane would do the same.

Everything we had been through these past couple of weeks had been magical. Like a fairytale. But it was also real life, and I was living the kind of amazing love story that I'd always been told didn't really exist.

But I knew for a fact that it did. And all these feelings we had experienced since we met had just been solidified by the fact that Thomas and Claire had finally found their happy ending, too.

Dane and I were completely in love. And this was just the beginning of our story.

Chapter 26

Thomas
One Month Later

ONCE EVERYTHING HAD worked out in my life, I felt like a young man again. I stood on the porch at the ranch, looking out over the fields, taking a deep breath of Montana air.

The cows were out in the field, the ranch hands taking care of fixing the fences before they headed home for the night.

I had already finished my duties for the day, the paperwork was up-to-date and the administrative details had been taken care of. The ranch was running smoothly, still the best ranch in Montana, carrying the Brown legacy on as it had for the past one hundred and fifty years.

I leaned forward, my arms resting on the railing.

The sun was starting to set and it looked like the world was on fire. There was a chill in the air, a sure sign that winter was coming closer. Soon, these hills were going to be covered with snow and the world would be transformed into a winter wonderland. But for now, fall was still here and everything was bright and beautiful.

I wore my boots and jeans with heavy flannel shirts under fleece lined jackets. I felt comfortable and warm in my clothes. I didn't feel like a pain-ridden old man anymore. Even though I would never be the man I had once been, and even though the war had taken a lot from me, it felt like I had gained so much in these past few weeks.

Inside the house, music started and I smiled. The song was familiar. It was a song that played at The Bell in London, all those years ago. I couldn't believe that she had found it.

Without even thinking, I started tapping my foot to it. The sound, the music that floated around me, took me back to the bar where I had met her. The woman of my dreams. The love of my life. So much had happened since then, but it had all come full circle now, hadn't it? Thanks to Amelia and Dane, I had found the woman I had always wanted to spend my life with. And everything in my life was better again. All the questions had been answered. All the misery had been wiped away. And even though we had lost a precious fifty years, I was finally happy again.

I reached for the cup of coffee on the railing. It was still steaming and I blew on the top before I took a sip. Freshly brewed coffee, dark and strong. Just how I liked it.

Setting the cup down again, I looked back over the fields. When I heard the front door open behind me, I smiled but didn't turn around. A moment later, I felt a hand graze up my back and down my arm, fingers intertwining with mine. Claire hugged me from behind, her cheek against my back, her arms wrapping around my waist.

"Hello, darling," I said to her.

She stepped behind me and looked up. Her gray hair had been pulled back into a bun and she wore light make-up. Her lips were soft pink, not the bright red she had worn when I met her, but this suited her just as much.

I reached for her, cupping her cheek. She was still the same, beautiful woman. Even though we had both gotten older, she hadn't changed, and in so many way she was still the same. I ran my thumb along her bottom lip, tracing the line of her smile. She had wrinkles in the corners of her eyes that fanned out when she smiled up at me. And her dark eyes were so filled with wisdom, with love and adoration, and a slew of other emotions I couldn't even begin to decipher.

She had always been like this. Studious, steadfast, stubborn even. But beautiful and elegant and gentle. And all of it was still there. She was still the most beautiful woman I had ever seen, the only woman I ever wanted to be with.

I was filled with love and joy.

"What are you thinking about, my English girl?" I asked.

She smiled and leaned against me. I put my arm around her shoulders and thought just how absolutely perfect this was.

"Just how lucky we are that we found each other," she said. When her head was against my shoulder like this, with me towering above her, everything was perfect. It was as if we had been made for each other. And even though we were a little older now, a little more worn, everything still fit exactly the way it should have.

"Lucky that they found us, you mean," I said.

She leaned against me. "Yes. I miss him."

Claire had always had a very good relationship with her grandson, Dane. And I understood why. He was a wonderful man, everything a man should be. When I had met him, I liked him right away. And even now, the more I got to know him, the more I liked him. He had integrity and honor and pride. And all the other important things a man should have to be able to make a good life and look after his woman.

"You'll see him again, soon," I promised, planting a kiss on Claire's forehead. "A few weeks at the very most."

Claire nodded and we both looked out over the fields. There is so much going on in my mind. It was beautiful looking out over the ranch. And it was a dream come true to have Claire here. But our story was a little more complicated. When Dane came to visit, Amelia would come with him. But so would a man called Junior. Reggie Junior. The man who was my son.

When Claire had told me that I was a father, I had been shocked. I'd never known that she was pregnant, and to think that she had been so terrified of her future alone with a baby to care for that she'd accepted a marriage to a man she didn't love had pained me deeply. But there was nothing that could be changed. I had grown up without knowing I had a son, and my son had grown up without knowing I even existed.

Claire had cried when she told me what she had done and why, and how it all turned out. She had apologized profusely, telling me that she knew it made her terrible person. But I had never seen it that way. The only thing I had seen when I looked at her tearstained face was a woman who had been so scared, she hadn't seen another way out. I understood where she had come from, why she had made the decisions that she had. Plus, she may not have survived had she stayed in London.

I only wished I could have been there for her, and that we could have raised our son together rather than her having to live a life that was so awful.

When Dane came, I was going to meet Reggie Junior for the first time. Dane was coming with his father so I could meet him. But that wasn't all that was happening. Dane was also going to bring a couple of Claire's items that she couldn't bring with her when she flew to Montana four nights ago.

"What's on your mind?" Claire asked, looking up at me again.

I shook my head. I didn't have to tell her about my fear of meeting my son, wondering if he was going to like me. She didn't need to know that I was nervous about that part. I didn't want her to feel even more guilty than she already did, or to start worrying about it again. Besides, we had so much going for us, and everything had gone well so far. It was only fair to believe that it would continue to do so.

"I'm just thinking how happy I am to finally have you here with me where you belong."

Claire turned to me and wrapped her arms around my waist, her head on my chest. Together, we watched the sunset.

This was what we had always dreamed of.

"Claire," I said, and she looked up at me, her chin on my chest, her dark eyes beautiful as ever. "I love you."

Her smile was as bright as the sun, her eyes crinkling at the corners and she stood on her toes to reach me. She pressed her lips against mine and heat washed through my body, the magic dancing on my skin. She had always done this, from the very moment we had kissed the first time. I had such a strong sense of déjà vu, ripped back to that night outside Westminster Abbey. This was the fairytale. This was the happy ending. This was what defined our relationship. Because nothing about us, not how we met, not how we separated, and not how we had found each other again, was something that anyone could have thought up. No, this was destiny. And sometimes, destiny led us down a road we could never imagine.

"I love you, too, Thomas Brown," Claire said.

She lowered herself again, and we stood together for the longest time. The sun set, with the pink and purple burning sky changing over to an inky black. Crickets started chirping in the fields beyond, and finally, it was time to go inside.

Chapter 27

Amelia

I STOOD BEHIND THE counter at the antique store. It was my normal morning routine, opening up the shop, going through the new inventory, and putting out furniture to attract visitors. I hummed as I worked, enjoying going through the motions. I loved routine, I loved stability.

And most of all, I loved being surrounded by history and everything that came to life with stories of days gone by.

After taking care of the shop itself, I walked to the counter where I had put a box that had arrived just this morning. It looked to be filled with trinkets and I was sure that I would find some interesting things in it. There were always interesting things coming into the shop when people came to drop off boxes of old goods they found in houses they cleaned out, or when they bought boxes in bulk.

When I started unpacking the box, I found a stack of books that would be great on the bookshelf, a journal with words that were hardly legible, and a jewelry box full with jewelry that could have wonderful stories behind it. These had to be polished, though.

At the bottom of the box was a small case. It was silver, engraved with beautiful floral designs. I picked it up and looked at it from all sides. When I opened it, a very old compass was inside. It looked handcrafted.

I opened the little lid. On the inside was an inscription, carved into the metal.

My love, I will always find my way back to you.

Arthur walked into the store.

"Good morning," he said, with a smile. "How are you today? Can you believe how busy we are? The store is suddenly the hotspot in town." He continued prattling on without waiting for me to answer any of his questions. "We've had so much business, I might have to hire an assistant to help you out."

Laughing, I turned to him. "I think that is a great idea. It's wonderful that we're so busy, now. Who would have known that history would be so interesting, eh?"

"Thanks to you," Arthur said. "If you hadn't published that story, none of this would have happened."

I smiled. I had asked Thomas and Claire if it was all right with them that I published their story. It was too amazing to die with them. I wanted the world to know how beautiful it was when lost love could be found again.

The story was called "Finding her American Soldier," and it followed me and Dane, working to find Claire and then Thomas, and finally reuniting the elderly couple.

I thought about the story, about everything Dane and I had been through. And if I had to be honest, I was itching for a new adventure. It had only been a month or so since Claire and Thomas had found each other again, but in that time, Dane and I had nothing to work on. Nothing like the love story that had united us.

Looking at the compass again, I turned it over in my hand, studying the fine craftsmanship.

"What do you have there?" Arthur asked.

"I found this at the bottom of the box," I said.

Arthur held out his hand and I passed it to him. He looked at it, his brows knitting together, his eyes narrowing.

"This is a real find, Amelia!" he cried out. "I'm thinking sixteen hundreds, if not earlier. It looks handmade."

I nodded. "I thought the same thing. We can't sell this one in the shop."

Arthur shook his head. "Definitely not. You're going to have to find a better home for it."

"Me?" I asked. Technically, everything that came into the shop belonged to Arthur by default. He was the shop owner and all donations went directly to him.

But Arthur nodded. "You found it, and based on my experience with what you do with the things you find, I think it's only right if you have it. Do with it what you see fit."

I smiled, excitement bubbling up inside me. Who knew what this could mean? I wanted to know where this compass had come from. I wanted to find out who had written the words inscribed on the inside, and how it had ended up here in the shop.

Maybe it would be a dead end. Maybe I wouldn't find out anything at all. After all, there wasn't a name like there had been in the letter. And Pinewood was such a small town. There was a chance that I wouldn't find anything at all. But what if I did? Imagine if it was another story like that of Thomas and Claire?

The bell above the door rang and our first customer walked in. It was an older woman and she headed straight for the bookshelf.

"I have a couple of books that just came in this morning," I said to her in passing. "If you don't find anything you like over there, you welcome to have a look and I can keep it aside for you once I get it logged into the system."

"Thank you, Amelia," she said. I didn't know who she was, but everyone around knew who I was, now. I had gained a little bit of fame after publishing the story, and I would be lying if I said I didn't like it.

Arthur nodded at me, a look of approval on his face. And didn't that just make me feel great? I liked that Arthur was happy with how things were going at store, and with how hard I was working. And if he appointed another worker at the shop, maybe I would be able to be a manager and get a little time off, time to explore and discover more stories.

But we would see. For now, I was happy exactly where I was, doing just what I loved.

Sirens sounded in the distance and we all looked toward the door. It didn't happen very often that the police were active in town, but there were times that things went wrong. The sirens grew louder and louder, as a car pulled up in front of the shop.

"What on earth?" Arthur asked.

Through the car's window, I could see Dane behind the wheel and a smile crept onto my face.

The speaker mounted onto the car squealed as Dane took the mic and spoke into it.

"Amelia, please get your fine rear end into the back of my vehicle, immediately," Dane said.

Not only did Arthur and our customer hear, but the whole street could hear it. Hell, the whole town would be able to hear it.

A blush crept onto my cheeks and I looked at Arthur.

"Oh, my goodness, I'm so sorry," I said. But I couldn't swallow back my laugh.

Arthur chuckled and shook his head. "It sounds like the police need you, Amelia. Maybe you should go ahead and do as they ask."

"Are you going to be fine here?" I asked.

"My dear, I ran the shop long before you came to work for me. I'm sure I can handle a couple of customers while you're gone. Go on, have some fun."

"Thank you," I said with a grin. I grabbed my bag from underneath the counter and headed toward the door. When I opened the car door and slid into the passenger seat, Dane looked at me with a stern expression. He looked so damn good in his uniform. His eyes were bright and his hair was a bit of a mess and everything about him was lively.

"I thought I told you to get in the back," he said.

I laughed. "Just drive, Romeo."

Just after Thomas and Claire had found each other, Dane had gone to see Chief Hopkins again. He had explained to him that he was in a better space, and even though there was no concrete proof of it, I was sure that Hopkins had been able to see the difference. Because two weeks later, Dane had been allowed back on the force. And since he had been back at work again, I could only see him getting better and better.

There were still times when he struggled, when he had nightmares about the shooting, or about Drew and not being able to save him. There were times when he struggled with anxiety or paranoia.

But he was getting so much better, and being back on the force, doing the one job he knew exactly how to do, was really good for him. It kept him busy, and they welcomed him back with open arms, as if he was the prodigal son returned.

It was good for him.

And because Dane was in a good space, and because I loved what I did, we were both incredibly happy. It was good for our relationship, too. Because Dane and I were now officially together.

As we drove through town, I could see people turning around and looking at us. Everyone knew that we were together now, too. In a town as small as Pinewood, it was impossible to hide things like that for very long. But the story I had written for the paper had also given everyone a hint.

Dane pulled up in front of the little ice cream shop.

"What's this?" I asked.

"We need sustenance for the road," he said.

He hopped out and came back with two ice creams, the same flavors we had ordered on our second date. As we drove, eating ice cream, I thought that life couldn't get any better.

Until I remembered the compass in my pocket.

"I found something," I said. I took the compass out and showed him. Dane stopped at a red light and looked at it.

"What is it?" he asked.

"It's a compass," I said. "Arthur thinks it could be from the sixteen hundreds, and we both believe it's handcrafted. It's a big deal. And there's an inscription inside."

"Oh, so it's something personal," Dane said.

I nodded. "I'm dying to find out where it came from and who it belonged to."

Dane glanced at me with a smile. "Have I told you how much I love the fact that you are so into history? You are such a nerd, and it's so hot."

I giggled. "Okay, that's great, but you are quite a nerd then, too. You're just as excited about these things as I am."

"Only if it holds an adventure, you know, like the last one."

I nodded. Dane wasn't as eager about history as I was, but when there was a story to be found, he was completely on board. And I loved that we could do things like that together, that he was as interested in it as I was. It would always be our thing, it was the reason why we had gotten so close.

"Well, this one might be nothing," I said. "It could be a dead end, and impossible to discover where it came from or who it belonged to."

"Or?" Dane asked, knowing that I wasn't done talking yet.

I looked at him, smiling, all the excitement bubbling up inside me again. This was what it was about. This was my relationship with Dane. Not only will we be there for each other through the hard times and the happy times, supporting each other, and getting to know each other inside and out. We were also going on adventures together, exploring part of the world and our lives that we had never seen before. And I wouldn't have it any other way. Dane was the person I wanted to share all of it with, my adventures, my interests, and every part of my life.

"Or," I said, reaching for Dane's hand on the stick shift, "it might be our next adventure."

THE END

War Torn Letter Series

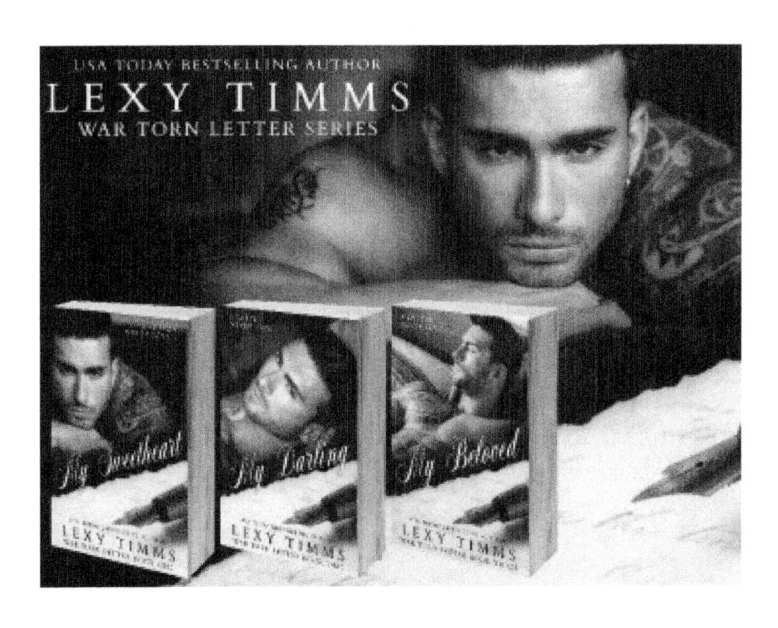

Learn from yesterday, live for today, hope for tomorrow. The important this is not to stop questioning.
Albert Einstein

My Sweetheart - Book 1
My Darling - Book 2
My Beloved – Book 3

Find Lexy Timms:

LEXY TIMMS NEWSLETTER:
http://eepurl.com/9i0vD
Lexy Timms Facebook Page:
https://www.facebook.com/SavingForever
Lexy Timms Website:
http://www.lexytimms.com

Want

FREE READS?

Sign up for Lexy Timms' newsletter
And she'll send you updates on new releases,
ARC copies of books and a whole lotta fun!

Sign up for news and updates!
http://eepurl.com/9i0vD

More by Lexy Timms:

FROM BEST SELLING AUTHOR, Lexy Timms, comes a billionaire romance that'll make you swoon and fall in love all over again.

Jamie Connors has given up on men. Despite being smart, pretty, and just slightly overweight, she's a magnet for the kind of guys that don't stay around.

Her sister's wedding is at the foreground of the family's attention. Jamie would be fine with it if her sister wasn't pressuring her to lose weight so she'll fit in the maid of honor dress, her mother would get off her case and her ex-boyfriend wasn't about to become her brother-in-law.

Determined to step out on her own, she accepts a PA position from billionaire Alex Reid. The job includes an apartment on his property and gets her out of living in her parents' basement.

Jamie must balance her life and somehow figure out how to manage her billionaire boss, without falling in love with him.

** The Boss is book 1 in the Managing the Bosses series. All your questions won't be answered in the first book. It may end on a cliff hanger.

For mature audiences only. There are adult situations, but this is a love story, NOT erotica.

FRAGILE TOUCH

"HIS BODY IS PERFECT. He's got this face that isn't just heart-melting but actually kind of exotic..."

Lillian Warren's life is just how she's designed it. She has a high-paying job working with celebrities and the elite, teaching them how to better organize their lives. She's on her own, the days quiet, but she likes it that way. Especially since she's still figuring out how to live with her recent diagnosis of Crohn's disease. Her cats keep her company, and she's not the least bit lonely.

Fun-loving personal trainer, Cayden, thinks his neighbor is a killjoy. He's only seen her a few times, and the woman looks like she needs a drink or three. He knows how to party and decides to invite her to over—if he can find her. What better way to impress her than take care of her overgrown yard? She proceeds to thank him by throwing up in his painstakingly-trimmed-to-perfection bushes.

Something about the fragile, mysterious woman captivates him.

Something about this rough-on-the-outside bear of a man attracts Lily, despite her heart warning her to tread carefully.

Faking It Description:

HE GROANED. THIS WAS torture. Being trapped in a room with a beautiful woman was just about every man's fantasy, but he had to remember that this was just pretend.

Allyson Smith has crushed on her boss for years, but never dared to make a move. When she finds herself without a date to her brother's upcoming wedding, Allyson tells her family one innocent white lie: that she's been dating her boss. Unfortunately, her boss discovers her lie, and insists on posing as her boyfriend to escort her to the wedding.

Playboy billionaire Dane Prescott always has a new heiress on his arm, but he can't get his assistant Allyson out of his head. He's fought his attraction to her, until he gets caught up in her scheme of a fake relationship.

One passionate weekend with the boss has Allyson Smith questioning everything she believes in. Falling for a wealthy playboy like Dane is against the rules, but if she's just faking it what's the harm?

Capturing Her Beauty

KAYLA REID HAS ALWAYS been into fashion and everything to do with it. Growing up wasn't easy for her. A bigger girl trying to squeeze

MY BELOVED

into the fashion world is like trying to suck an entire gelatin mold through a straw; possible, but difficult.

She found herself an open door as a designer and jumped right in. Her designs always made the models smile. The colors, the fabrics, the styles. Never once did she dream of being on the other side of the lens. She got to watch her clothing strut around on others and that was good enough.

But who says you can't have a little fun when you're off the clock?

Sometimes trying on the latest fashions is just as good as making them. Kayla's hours in front of the mirror were a guilty pleasure.

A chance meeting with one of the company photographers may turn into more than just an impromptu photo shoot.

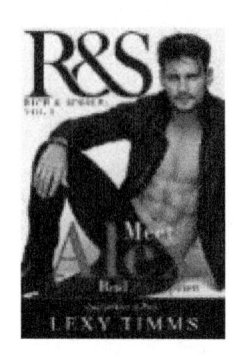

Hot n' Handsome, Rich & Single... how far are you willing to go?
MEET ALEX REID, CEO of Reid Enterprise. Billionaire extraordinaire, chiseled to perfection, panty-melter and currently single.

Learn about Alex Reid before he began Managing the Bosses. Alex Reid sits down for an interview with R&S.

His lifestyle is like his handsome looks: hard, fast, breath-taking and out to play ball. He's risky, charming and determined.

How close to the edge is Alex willing to go? Will he stop at nothing to get what he wants?

Alex Reid is book 1 in the R&S Rich and Single Series. Fall in love with these hot and steamy men; all single, successful, and searching for love.

Book One is FREE!
SOMETIMES THE HEART needs a different kind of saving... find out if Charity Thompson will find a way of saving forever in this hospital setting Best-Selling Romance by Lexy Timms

MY BELOVED

Charity Thompson wants to save the world, one hospital at a time. Instead of finishing med school to become a doctor, she chooses a different path and raises money for hospitals – new wings, equipment, whatever they need. Except there is one hospital she would be happy to never set foot in again—her fathers. So of course, he hires her to create a gala for his sixty-fifth birthday. Charity can't say no. Now she is working in the one place she doesn't want to be. Except she's attracted to Dr. Elijah Bennet, the handsome playboy chief.

Will she ever prove to her father that's she's more than a med school dropout? Or will her attraction to Elijah keep her from repairing the one thing she desperately wants to fix?

HEART OF THE BATTLE Series

In a world plagued with darkness, she would be his salvation.

No one gave Erik a choice as to whether he would fight or not. Duty to the crown belonged to him, his father's legacy remaining beyond the grave.

Taken by the beauty of the countryside surrounding her, Linzi would do anything to protect her father's land. Britain is under attack and Scotland is next. At a time she should be focused on suitors, the men of her country have gone to war and she's left to stand alone.

Love will become available, but will passion at the touch of the enemy unravel her strong hold first?

THE RECRUITING TRIP

Aspiring college athlete Aileen Nessa is finding the recruiting process beyond daunting. Being ranked #10 in the world for the 100m hurdles at the age of eighteen is not a fluke, even though she believes that one race, where everything clicked magically together, might be. American universities don't seem to think so. Letters are pouring in from all over the country.

As she faces the challenge of differentiating between a college's genuine commitment to her or just empty promises from talent-seeking coaches, Aileen heads to the University of Gatica, a Division One school, on a recruiting trip. Her best friend dares her to go just to see the cute guys on the school's brochure.

The university's athletic program boasts one of the top hurdlers in the country. Tyler Jensen is the school's NCAA champion in the hurdles and Jim Thorpe recipient for top defensive back in football. His incredible blue-green eyes, confident smile and rock hard six pack abs mess with Aileen's concentration.

His offer to take her under his wing, should she choose to come to Gatica, is a temping proposition that has her wondering if she might be with an angel or making a deal with the devil himself.

THE ONE YOU CAN'T FORGET

Emily Rose Dougherty is a good Catholic girl from mythical Walkerville, CT. She had somehow managed to get herself into a heap trouble with the law, all because an ex-boyfriend has decided to make things difficult.

Luke "Spade" Wade owns a Motorcycle repair shop and is the Road Captain for Hades' Spawn MC. He's shocked when he reads in the paper that his old high school flame has been arrested. She's always been the one he couldn't forget.

Will destiny let them find each other again? Or what happened in the past, best left for the history books?

** *This is book 1 of the Hades' Spawn MC Series. All your questions may not be answered in the first book.*

BILLIONAIRE BIKER
LEXY TIMMS
Download For
FREE
Lexy
Timms

HOUSE
ROMANCE
CAUGHT
FLAMES
BESTSELLING AUTHOR
LEXY TIMMS
LIMITED
TIME
Lexy
Timms
FREE
DOWNLOAD

ONE YOU CAN'T
Forget
LEXY TIMMS
Lexy
Timms
Grab Your
FREE
Copy Today!

Lexy
Timms
THE BOSS
Managing the Bosses: Book 1
Lexy
Timms
Grab your
copy today!

Lexy
Timms
FOREVER
BOOK 3
BOOK 2
BOOK 1
Saving
FOREVER
Lexy
Timms
Limited
Time for
99cents

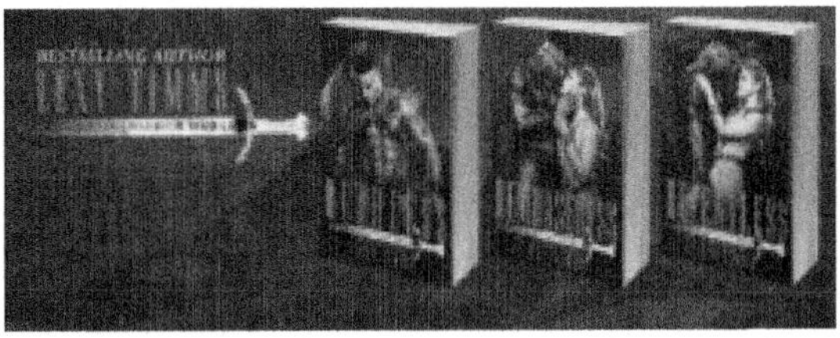

Bestselling Author
LEXY TIMMS
BEATING THE Biker

LEXY TIMMS
MOMENT IN TIME: BOOK ONE
HIGHLANDERS
Bride

Also by Lexy Timms

A Bad Boy Bullied Romance
I Hate You

A Burning Love Series
Spark of Passion
Flame of Desire
Blaze of Ecstasy

A Chance at Forever Series
Forever Perfect
Forever Desired
Forever Together

A "Kind of" Billionaire
Taking a Risk
Safety in Numbers
Pretend You're Mine

BBW Romance Series
Capturing Her Beauty
Pursuing Her Dreams
Tracing Her Curves

Beating the Biker Series
Making Her His
Making the Break
Making of Them

Billionaire Banker Series
Banking on Him
Price of Passion
Investing in Love
Knowing Your Worth
Treasured Forever
Banking on Christmas

Billionaire Holiday Romance Series
Driving Home for Christmas
The Valentine Getaway
Cruising Love

Billionaire in Disguise Series

Facade
Illusion
Charade

Billionaire Secrets Series
The Secret
Freedom
Courage
Trust
Impulse
Billionaire Secrets Box Set Books #1-3

Branded Series
Money or Nothing
What People Say
Give and Take

Building Billions
Building Billions - Part 1
Building Billions - Part 2
Building Billions - Part 3

Change of Heart Series
The Heart Needs
The Heart Wants
The Heart Knows

Conquering Warrior Series
Ruthless

Counting the Billions
Counting the Days
Counting On You
Counting the Kisses

Diamond in the Rough Anthology
Billionaire Rock
Billionaire Rock - part 2

Dominating PA Series
Her Personal Assistant - Part 1
Her Personal Assistant Box Set

Fake Billionaire Series
Faking It
Temporary CEO
Caught in the Act
Never Tell A Lie
Fake Christmas
Fake Billionaire Box Set #1-3

Firehouse Romance Series
Caught in Flames
Burning With Desire
Craving the Heat
Firehouse Romance Complete Collection

For His Pleasure
Elizabeth
Georgia
Madison

Fortune Riders MC Series
Billionaire Biker
Billionaire Ransom
Billionaire Misery

Fragile Series
Fragile Touch
Fragile Kiss
Fragile Love

Hades' Spawn Motorcycle Club
One You Can't Forget
One That Got Away

One That Came Back
One You Never Leave
One Christmas Night
Hades' Spawn MC Complete Series

Hard Rocked Series
Rhyme
Harmony
Lyrics

Heart of Stone Series
The Protector
The Guardian
The Warrior

Heart of the Battle Series
Celtic Viking
Celtic Rune
Celtic Mann
Heart of the Battle Series Box Set

Heistdom Series
Master Thief
Goldmine
Diamond Heist
Smile For Me

Highlander Wolf Series
Pack Run
Pack Land
Pack Rules

Just About Series
About Love
About Truth
About Forever

Justice Series
Seeking Justice
Finding Justice
Chasing Justice
Pursuing Justice
Justice - Complete Series

Kissed by Billions
Kissed by Passion
Kissed by Desire
Kissed by Love

Love You Series
Love Life

Need Love
My Love

Managing the Billionaire
Never Enough
Worth the Cost
Secret Admirers
Chasing Affection
Pressing Romance
Timeless Memories

Managing the Bosses Series
The Boss
The Boss Too
Who's the Boss Now
Love the Boss
I Do the Boss
Wife to the Boss
Employed by the Boss
Brother to the Boss
Senior Advisor to the Boss
Forever the Boss
Christmas With the Boss
Billionaire in Control
Billionaire Makes Millions
Billionaire at Work
Precious Little Thing
Priceless Love
Gift for the Boss - Novella 3.5
Managing the Bosses Box Set #1-3

Model Mayhem Series
Shameless
Modesty
Imperfection

Moment in Time
Highlander's Bride
Victorian Bride
Modern Day Bride
A Royal Bride
Forever the Bride

My Best Friend's Sister
Hometown Calling
A Perfect Moment
Thrown in Together

Neverending Dream Series
Neverending Dream - Part 1
Neverending Dream - Part 2
Neverending Dream - Part 3
Neverending Dream - Part 4
Neverending Dream - Part 5

Outside the Octagon
Submit
Fight
Knockout

Protecting Diana Series
Her Bodyguard
Her Defender
Her Champion
Her Protector
Her Forever

Protecting Layla Series
His Mission
His Objective
His Devotion

Racing Hearts Series
Rush
Pace
Fast

Reverse Harem Series
Primals

Archaic
Unitary

RIP Series
Track the Ripper
Hunt the Ripper
Pursue the Ripper

R&S Rich and Single Series
Alex Reid
Parker

Saving Forever
Saving Forever - Part 1
Saving Forever - Part 2
Saving Forever - Part 3
Saving Forever - Part 4
Saving Forever - Part 5
Saving Forever - Part 6
Saving Forever Part 7
Saving Forever - Part 8
Saving Forever Boxset Books #1-3

Shifting Desires Series
Jungle Heat
Jungle Fever

Jungle Blaze

Southern Romance Series
Little Love Affair
Siege of the Heart
Freedom Forever
Soldier's Fortune

Spanked Series
Passion
Playmate
Pleasure

Spelling Love Series
The Author
The Book Boyfriend
The Words of Love

Taboo Wedding Series
He Loves Me Not
With This Ring
Happily Ever After

Tattooist Series

Confession of a Tattooist
Surrender of a Tattooist
Heart of a Tattooist
Hopes & Dreams of a Tattooist

Tennessee Romance
Whisky Lullaby
Whisky Melody
Whisky Harmony

The Bad Boy Alpha Club
Battle Lines - Part 1
Battle Lines

The Brush Of Love Series
Every Night
Every Day
Every Time
Every Way
Every Touch

The Debt
The Debt: Part 1 - Damn Horse
The Debt: Complete Collection

The Fire Inside Series
Dare Me
Defy Me
Burn Me

The Golden Mail
Hot Off the Press
Extra! Extra!
Read All About It
Stop the Press
Breaking News
This Just In

The Lucky Billionaire Series
Lucky Break
Streak of Luck
Lucky in Love

The Sound of Breaking Hearts Series
Disruption
Destroy
Devoted

The University of Gatica Series

The Recruiting Trip
Faster
Higher
Stronger
Dominate
No Rush
University of Gatica - The Complete Series

T.N.T. Series
Troubled Nate Thomas - Part 1
Troubled Nate Thomas - Part 2
Troubled Nate Thomas - Part 3

Undercover Series
Perfect For Me
Perfect For You
Perfect For Us

Unknown Identity Series
Unknown
Unpublished
Unexposed
Unsure
Unwritten
Unknown Identity Box Set: Books #1-3

Unlucky Series
Unlucky in Love
UnWanted
UnLoved Forever

War Torn Letters Series
My Sweetheart
My Darling
My Beloved

Wet & Wild Series
Stormy Love
Savage Love
Secure Love

Worth It Series
Worth Billions
Worth Every Cent
Worth More Than Money

You & Me - A Bad Boy Romance
Just Me
Touch Me
Kiss Me

Standalone
Wash
Loving Charity
Summer Lovin'
Love & College
Billionaire Heart
First Love
Frisky and Fun Romance Box Collection
Beating Hades' Bikers

Watch for more at www.lexytimms.com.

About the Author

"Love should be something that lasts forever, not is lost forever." Visit USA TODAY BESTSELLING AUTHOR, LEXY TIMMS https://www.facebook.com/SavingForever *Please feel free to connect with me and share your comments. I love connecting with my readers.* Sign up for news and updates and freebies - I like spoiling my readers! http://eepurl.com/9i0vD website: www.lexytimms.com Dealing in Antique Jewelry and hanging out with her awesome hubby and three kids, Lexy Timms loves writing in her free time. MANAGING THE BOSSES is a bestselling 10-part series dipping into the lives of Alex Reid and Jamie Connors. Can a secretary really fall for her billionaire boss?

Read more at www.lexytimms.com.

Printed in Great Britain
by Amazon